BROKEN SILENCE

ANNSLEE URBAN

D0650929

HARLEQUIN® LOVE INSPIRED® SUSPENSE

Recycling programs
for this product may
not exist in your area.

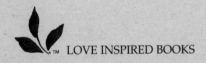

LOVE INSPIRED BOOKS

ISBN-13: 978-0-373-44658-2

Broken Silence

www.Harlequin.com

Printed in U.S.A.

Be strong and courageous. Do not be afraid or terrified because of them, for the Lord your God goes with you; He will never leave you nor forsake you.
–Deuteronomy 31:6

This book is lovingly dedicated to
my three beautiful daughters: Gina, Andrea and Olivia.
You are among my greatest blessings and my inspiration.

And to my Grandkiddos: Cameron, Isaac, Jayce and Kaylee,
who are a constant reminder of God's wonder and grace.

Also a special thanks to my editor, Shana Asaro,
and my agent, Mary Sue Seymour. Thank you for all you do.
It is a privilege and blessing to work with you.

And most of all I thank my heavenly Father
for making this dream come true.

ONE

The distant toll of the Chatham County, Georgia, clock tower rang twelve noon as Amber Talbot left the Safe Harbor Counseling Center and headed down River Street to her car.

The forecast had called for late-afternoon thunderstorms here in Savannah, but already dark clouds hovered low in the sky. A rising breeze swept the tree-lined streets, rustling spring foliage and delivering a sudden chill to the air. Turning up her collar, Amber eyed the murky waves that boomed against wooden docks. Boats tied to their posts bobbed like corks in the water. Curling whitecaps crashed over their bows.

Amber pulled in a breath of humid air and picked up her pace. Perfect weather to snuggle up with a good book. Exactly what she needed. After weeks of being bogged down at work, she was treating herself to a restful weekend.

With those thoughts echoing in her head, Amber jogged up a short flight of steps to the parking lot. Lengthening her strides, she dug out her key fob and unlocked her car with a *click*.

"Ma'am, did you drop this?"

Amber spun in the direction of the male voice and found an older gentleman waving a manila envelope with her name sprawled across it.

She glanced at her open messenger bag, crammed full with her purse, client files and notes for her fund-raiser. How careless, she chastised herself, for forgetting to zip it closed.

Tucking the bag under her arm, she started toward the man. "Thank you, sir—"

A deafening blast filled the air.

Amber flew backward, landed hard on the pavement. Black smoke plumed in front of her. The ground shook as glass and metal rained down like a hailstorm. Scrambling to her knees, she hurled her arms over her head to protect it from the shower of stinging objects. A *whoosh* sounded, then she heard crackling as heat blanketed her. She willed herself to move but couldn't.

I'm going to die!

"Lady, are you okay?" The man's distant shriek filled her ears. "You need to get away from the flames!"

Amber's body pulsed with pain. Smoke raked across her eyes like claws. She squeezed them shut as coughs racked her lungs. She pulled herself forward, crawling in the direction of the man's voice. Shrapnel bit into her palms and knees, but adrenaline kept her moving until the man grabbed her arm and yanked her to her feet.

"I called 9-1-1. Help's on the way," the older man screeched between hacks. "Was that your car?"

Amber's lungs burned. She worked to breathe. On shaky legs she managed to turn.

The smoke had subsided some, but the car was engulfed in flames. Panic grew; her mind spun with shock.

"Yes," she said, disbelieving. "That *was* my car."

"Possible car bomb off River Street," the police radio blared.

Detective Patrick Wiley forgot about the lunch meeting with his boss, swung his SUV around and headed that way.

His years as a navy SEAL had taught him one thing: get to the scene when the evidence was fresh. Facts and data meant a lot when he put his senses to the test.

Pulling a small siren from under his seat, he slapped it on the roof of the vehicle and sped onto the Talmadge Memorial Bridge. Cars swerved out of his way, and in moments he was over the Savannah River and nearing River Street.

He knew about car bombings—shrapnel, flying debris, collateral damage, innocent bloodshed. A coward's weapon of destruction.

Unlike his days in Afghanistan, this, he surmised, was likely faulty mechanic work resulting in an engine fire.

He came to a stop at the scene and leaped from his car. His positive rationale faded, and a dire feeling settled in his gut. Dark smoke blanketed the sky, the smell of destruction in the air. Rescue vehicles crammed into the small parking lot. Lines of fire hoses snaked every which way from multiple trucks.

Fortunately the parking lot hadn't been full. The tourist season had yet to take off, due to the looming storm and cooler-than-usual spring temperatures. A blessing in disguise, as it turned out.

Patrick wove his way around rescue and police vehicles, moving closer to the scene. Firefighters battled the last of the flames biting at the charred skeleton of the small sedan. A dozen yards away, paramedics tended to a young woman sitting in the back of an ambulance.

He gave another assessing glance of the area. No other casualties came into view.

Lightning flashed in the distance, followed by a clap of thunder. Hopefully the forensics team could collect any evidence before the storm hit.

Officer Bill Robinson hurried toward him, stepping around the tangle of hoses. "That was some explosion.

We got calls from folks who felt it ten blocks away." He jerked his head toward the woman sitting in the back of an EMS vehicle. "Somebody really wanted that girl scared, or dead."

By the looks of the damage and scattered debris, Patrick didn't doubt it. "Is she the only victim?"

"As far as we can tell," Bill said, taking off his hat and shaking his head. "She was fortunate. If she hadn't dropped something and went back to get it…" He didn't finish, just wagged his head.

Patrick got the picture. "Did she give you any information about who might be responsible?"

Bill shook his head again. "Shocked and confused is all I got out of her. She's pretty cut up, too. Probably needs a little time to process everything."

"I'll talk to her and see what I can find out." Patrick patted Bill on the shoulder, then made his way to the ambulance.

As a paramedic cleaned the wounds on Amber's hands, she watched firefighters douse the remaining flames from her car until the charred piece of metal smoldered. Nausea rolled through her abdomen. Forty-eight months of payments up in smoke. Literally.

Amber drew a deep breath. *What am I thinking?* At least she hadn't been in it.

"You really need to get to the ER," the paramedic reiterated for the fourth time.

She clenched her fist against the sting of alcohol and settled her gaze back on the man. "Do you think I'll need stitches?"

"You've got some pretty good lacerations on your hands and knees. If nothing else, you'll need to get a tetanus shot."

Amber looked at her palms and grimaced. The bloody

gouges in her flesh looked as painful as they felt. "I'd really like to just go home. A hot shower and antibiotic cream sounds more appealing than a trip to the ER."

"Your call, but I wouldn't recommend it."

Of course not. She stretched out one leg and winced. Then glanced at her hands again. He probably was right. "Okay. I suppose I should go."

"Great. We'll get packed and be on our way. Since you're stable, you can buckle up where you are on the bench seat. We won't need to strap you onto the gurney."

"I really appreciate that." More than he could imagine.

Still, the mere thought of the ambulance ride made her uneasy. It was something she'd never wanted to experience again. Let alone a trip to the emergency room. She flexed her fingers and cringed against the pain. She was being ridiculous. Nearly a decade had passed. The nightmares had faded.

But the memories lingered—along with the guilt.

"Ma'am, could I speak to you for a moment?" The rich deep timbre of the man's voice raised goose bumps along her arms.

She jerked her head up, and her breath caught as a tall figure stepped to the door of the EMS vehicle. Broad and muscular, he had a bewildered look on his face that probably mimicked her own. "Patrick?"

"Amber?" Patrick cocked his head to the side, his dark, velvety eyes and strong, chiseled features as intriguing as ever. Little had changed over the past eleven years. If anything the years had only enhanced his good looks.

"I sure wasn't expecting to find you here." The glint in his brown gaze was unexpectedly warm. So unlike the last time she'd seen him.

Ditto. She swallowed. "I didn't know you were back in town."

"Got home about a year ago. I work with the Savannah-

Chatham police department violent crimes unit." He flashed his badge, very detectivelike. "How are you?"

"Happy to be alive." She tried for a smile, but hated that just the sight of him caused her pulse to rev. He shouldn't have that effect on her, especially after all she'd put him through. Her guilt alone should have tamped those emotions years ago.

"I'm sure you are happy to be alive. That was a pretty violent explosion." Patrick gestured to the remains of her car. "Who do you think did this?"

Shaking her head, she shrugged. "No idea. Maybe a random act. I don't know."

His head moved in an agreeable nod, but she could just imagine his churning thoughts. He didn't buy it. He hadn't changed one iota. Always suspected the worst. Still, she held on to the hope that her car had been a random choice by some wayward lunatic.

Patrick turned his head and stared back at the charred debris. "Did you see anyone in the parking lot or notice anything unusual before the bomb went off?"

"No. The parking lot was nearly empty. With the storm approaching, this area of town has been pretty deserted."

His gaze met hers again, his eyes narrowing. "What about the man who found the item you dropped?"

"I dropped a file on the sidewalk leading to the parking area. Thankfully, that gentleman was around, otherwise—" Amber choked on the last word, suddenly dizzy. She could have been killed.

"Detective, are you about finished with your questions?" the medic asked as he placed the orange plastic supply box into the back of the emergency vehicle.

"For now." Patrick gave the medic a nod, then returned his attention to Amber. "I'll let you get to the hospital and catch up with you later." He pulled a card from his wallet and handed it to her. "Call me if any new revelations come to you."

Amber took the card, breathing relief when the paramedic closed the doors. A siren roared and the ambulance maneuvered out of the tight parking lot. She lolled her head back against the vinyl seat, ignoring the pain streaking through her extremities. Tears welled in her eyes just before she squeezed them shut.

This was definitely not her day.

Patrick watched the ambulance ease through the crowded parking lot and then pull away. Catching his breath, he felt his insides reel from the sucker punch that caught him the moment Amber's crystal-green gaze collided with his.

She hadn't changed at all. Sill had the same delicate features—straight little nose, high cheekbones, luscious full lips. And a tumble of dark mahogany curls, soft and flowing about her shoulders.

She was still mesmerizing.

Seeing her had unearthed a whole host of emotions he had no business feeling, given their history. Feelings he'd thought he'd buried the night she'd walked out of his life the summer after their freshman year of college. Just weeks after she'd accepted his ring.

Waves of emotion shuddered through Patrick as memories of Amber flooded his mind. Sweet memories still outnumbered the bad, which made seeing her sting that much more. Crazy, he thought. It had been eleven years.

He tilted his head back and deeply inhaled, trying to calm the turbulent pulsing in his veins. Instead, adrenaline kicked him into overdrive as the stench of smoke entered his lungs. He stiffened his posture. Refocused. This was not the time to deal with the irrational emotions knotting his gut. Someone had blown up a car. Amber may have been the target.

He had a crime to solve.

The next five hours passed in a blur. Amber sat on the edge of a stretcher in the ER and studied her hands wrapped in gauze. She wiggled her fingers. Tender but tolerable. Somehow not seeing the wounds made them smart less.

Not so with her legs. She straightened one. The wounds had been cleaned and left open to air, with several jagged stitches on each knee. The black tights she'd been wearing had offered nothing in the way of protection, as the deep abrasions on her now-bare legs attested. Not pretty and painfully sore.

The events of the day still struck her as surreal, even impossible. Why would someone plant a bomb in a nearly deserted parking lot?

In her car?

Thoughts tumbled around her mind, but no answers emerged. Amber rubbed a knuckle against the pounding in her temple, where a tension headache had taken hold. She'd grown up in Savannah. It was the one place she felt safe.

Until today.

A nurse walked into the room carrying a small syringe. She pulled gloves from a box mounted on the wall. "After I give you this tetanus shot, you'll be ready for discharge."

"Thank you." Amber nodded, happy to be nearing the end of her visit. Although her dreaded time in the emergency room hadn't been as difficult as she'd imagined in terms of invoking memories.

A near miss with a bomb had taken care of that.

Her blood chilled at the thought.

"Right arm, please." The nurse pulled off the plastic tip of the syringe.

Amber flinched a little as the nurse gave her the shot.

"It may be sore for a few days, so just use a warm compress for the pain. I'll be right back with your paperwork." The nurse left the room.

The pain from a tiny shot was the least of Amber's concerns.

"How about a ride home?"

At the sound of the deep voice, every fine hair on her neck rose to attention. She glanced up. Detective Patrick Wiley stood there, his commanding presence filling the doorway, his hands in the pockets of his leather jacket and one shoulder leaning against the door frame.

"A ride?" Amber blurted, startled more than she was surprised to see him again. She'd thought he'd wait at least until she got home and settled.

"The hospital called and said you were ready to be released."

Amber instinctively tucked a stray curl behind her ear. The sooty film on her hair reminded her how terrible she must look, while Patrick stood there looking…well, incredible. "Someone from the hospital called you?" She barely kept her voice from cracking. She sat up straighter, trying to look somewhat together, although after the day she had, she could hardly be expected to look calm and collected. It wasn't every day a bomb blew up her car, or Patrick Wiley popped back into her life.

He nodded. "I asked them to. I still have a few questions. So if you haven't called for a ride already, I can give you one."

Hesitating, Amber scoured her brain for an excuse. Then again, what excuse could she have? She hadn't called anyone. She blew out a breath. "Okay…if you don't mind."

"I'm ready whenever you are."

Which would be never.

Patrick pulled keys from his pocket and Amber blinked.

The man at the door was not just her old boyfriend, he was a law enforcement officer, here to do his job. That truth alone should have calmed her.

Instead, a fresh burst of regret exploded in her chest. Regret for choices she'd made and the results they'd caused.

Patrick pulled his SUV to the curb in front of Amber's wood-frame bungalow and killed the engine. Gusty wind whistled and raindrops pelted the windshield, punctuating the awkward silence that had settled in the air between them.

As eager as Patrick was to jump-start the investigation, he could tell Amber was still shell-shocked. Even as he'd updated her on the bomb squad's initial report for the explosives involved in the blast, she'd stayed rather apathetic, acknowledging his comments with a nod, but not saying much else. He had hoped to engage in a fact-finding conversation, but so far, that was not happening.

And after he spent two solid hours at the station poring over data collected at the crime scene, he realized very quickly that this wasn't going to be a slam-dunk investigation. And, as with most crimes of this magnitude, time was of the essence, meaning, like it or not, he needed to dig more into Amber's personal life.

Patrick flicked on the car's interior lights. He twisted in his seat and rested his arm on the center console. Not an easy feat for his large frame, but he wanted to give Amber his full attention. "I need to ask a few questions about your relationships. Is there anyone, in the past or presently, who might be nursing a grudge of some kind? Ex-boyfriend, spouse or otherwise."

She took a deep, silent breath. "Well, I've never had a spouse, and I can't think of any looming relationship issues."

Good. Not that it had any bearing on him personally,

but it might make working with her a little less awkward. "How about outstanding debt? Do you owe anybody anything?"

She shook her head. "No, I live pretty frugally. Other than my house, I'm debt-free. Well," she amended, "I guess I'll be buying a new car."

Patrick caught the subtle tremble of her body, but she kept any emotion off her face. He admired the way she was trying to stay strong, but he got a knot in his gut thinking about what she'd been through. A need to comfort her welled up inside of him.

He quickly stifled the impulse to pull her into his arms and offer her support. That wasn't his place anymore.

"I'm sorry about your car." His eyes captured hers, hoping to provide some solace, yet feeling ineffective against any stress she was dealing with.

"Thank you."

He shook his head, thinking back to the destruction the bomb had left. "It was only by God's grace that you made it out alive."

As Amber acknowledged his remark with a small nod, her gaze drifted away to the storm raging outside. "Yes, things could have been much worse."

It wasn't just her averted eyes, but the fleeting look of remorse tightening her features that made him wonder what kind of storm was raging inside her.

Patrick hesitated, giving her a moment. "Amber, are you okay?"

She returned her gaze to him, shapely brows drawn together. "Sorry. It's been a crazy day." She pushed hair from her face. "Are you finished with your questions?"

"No, I have a few more." Patrick shifted in the seat and switched modes, turning his focus once again on solving this case. "You talked about recently opening a counseling center. What kind of clients do you cater to?"

At the mention of her place of business, she brightened some. "Well, I work with two other counselors and we offer a variety of services, geared mostly toward women in crisis situations. We deal with everything from marital and family discord to substance abuse and mental health issues."

Patrick nodded to himself. "Okay, how about a family member or significant other of one of your clients—anyone seeking revenge for your intervention?"

Amber hesitated, brushing another stray lock of hair from her cheek. "It's possible, I guess. But most of my referrals come from the women's shelter or hospital social workers. It's a very confidential climate. I stay pretty much under the radar."

"I understand," Patrick said, although he did not completely dismiss the theory. "Have you received any unusual phone calls or messages lately?"

She shook her head. "No. Not that I can think of."

"How about someone threatening harm or making you feel unsafe?"

There was a short pause as she folded her hands in her lap. "No."

Patrick lifted a brow. "No one?"

She shook her head again.

Patrick gestured toward her house. "Do you feel safe staying here alone?"

Amber cast him a cool look, her eyes glinting amid the dim glow of the car's interior lights. "Why wouldn't I feel safe? You said yourself the bomb was crudely made. The work of an amateur."

"Amateur or not, someone planted it. In your car."

"In an almost empty lot." Her tone took on a bit of a defensive tenor. "I understand, Patrick, that it's your job to consider every angle. But I can't imagine anyone targeting me."

He nodded, hoping she was right.

A moment passed between them. Amber fiddled with her bag, and he was close enough to feel her discomfort.

She'd had a rough day and probably enough questions. "I think you've answered everything for tonight. Let me get an umbrella and walk you to your door." As Patrick reached into the backseat, his arm brushed hers. Something in the way she pulled away made a shiver run down his back.

"Thank you, Patrick. I really appreciate the ride, but I can see myself in."

Before he could remind her of the pouring rain, she jumped out of the vehicle and scampered down the sidewalk, her jacket pulled over her head.

He stared after her, waiting until she disappeared inside the house, the front door closing behind her.

She was hiding something.

A couple of fragmented thoughts pushed through the fog in his head. None of which had anything to do with a car bomb.

He had to stop himself. If he gave in to the urge to march to her door and ask a few questions, he'd be treading on unprofessional territory.

Patrick took a deep, bracing breath and started the engine. Personal issues would have to wait.

Soaking wet, Amber slumped against the door, her ears still ringing from the explosion, her knees throbbing. Not the best start to her weekend.

Seeing Patrick again definitely didn't help.

Taking a shaky breath, she turned around and engaged the dead bolt. She heard Patrick's SUV start up. The loud engine noise melded with the steady downpour. She waited a moment more until only the remnants of the storm filled her ears. Patrick was gone.

The one man in the world she never wanted to see again.

And here he was, the investigator for a crime that she, unfortunately, had gotten pulled into. Professionally polite, professionally impersonal, giving her no indication if he'd grown to forgive her or despise her for what she'd done.

Her mind wanted to go numb with the memories of the last time she'd seen him. The wounded look in his eyes when she'd told him she wasn't ready to commit. She'd needed time. She'd needed space. He hadn't responded well. Not that she'd expected him to.

That day she'd held him for the last time. Walked away. Grieved every step.

She'd made a sacrifice, penance for a mistake he couldn't understand.

Painful memories stabbed her, sending an icy shiver up her spine. Skin pebbling, she squeezed her eyes shut to block them, but instead more memories flooded in, and with them came the grief.

Indescribable grief that clung to her spirit was as fresh now as the night an unknown assailant had brutally attacked, drugged and attempted to rape her.

Although another student's intervention had halted her attacker's plans, her honor and dignity would remain tarnished. Forever.

Amber expelled a sharp sigh.

She had no one to blame but herself.

Patrick had warned her about the campus parties. But with him attending college on the other side of the state, she'd assumed he was being protective. And as her freshman year had neared the end, curiosity and boredom had outweighed good sense and she'd accepted a roommate's invitation to attend an end-of-the-year bash at a local fraternity.

The repercussions of that choice had changed the course of her dreams and sent her life spiraling into a sea of shame and regret.

No! Not tonight! Amber's jaw tightened as she willed the memories to cease.

Just thinking about the past, about Patrick, made her crazy. Especially since the path she'd paved for herself could never be erased.

Amber blinked back tears. She wouldn't cry. She refused to wallow in self-pity.

Lifting her chin, she hung her coat on a hook by the door and then trudged to the bedroom and dropped her bag on the floor. Her chest heaved with exhaustion. A shower might relax her and then maybe she could sleep. What she needed was a new day. Fresh thoughts.

Twenty minutes later, she crawled into bed, closed her eyes and tried to get comfortable while listening to the gentle howl of the wind and the last remnants of the rain patter on the window. Even as every fiber of her being cried for rest, insomnia settled in.

Time crawled, ticking unhurriedly in the darkness. The storm outside abated, leaving the shadows, the room, the air around her draped in a cold and eerie silence. Peace and quiet used to be a commodity she yearned for. But tonight it seemed more of a paradox than a possibility as thoughts of car bombs and explosions, of the upcoming charity fund-raiser and even Patrick Wiley wrestled in her mind.

Amber sat up, pumped her pillow, curled it into a ball and stuffed it back under her head. Okay, especially Patrick Wiley.

Emitting a groan, she wrenched up the blankets and pushed the disturbing thoughts aside, allowing pleasant ones to fill her mind.

Moments trickled by and finally her body and mind started to unwind. Her eyelids grew heavy and at last sleep pulled her in.

From the corner of her eye, she caught a movement.

She jerked her head. Eyes flickered back at her from the shadows.

"Amber." His voice was low, distorted.

Goose bumps pebbled her skin. "Who's there?"

"The man of your dreams." His low, chilling laughter echoed in the small space.

Dark. Claustrophobic. Panic stole her next breath. She needed to run. Needed to get out of there.

"Where's Boy Wonder now?" The man gave another laugh, his booted footsteps moving closer. "Who's going to save you now, Amber?"

Dread building, a scream rose in her throat. She tried to run, to get away...

Amber shot up with a gasp, her breathing short and rapid as her heart pounded like a sledgehammer in her chest.

Where am I?

Trembling, she sat there, chilled and clammy with sweat, her mind spinning. For long seconds she worked to steady her breathing, control the adrenaline pumping through her.

Her pulse slowed as reality trickled in.

It was just a dream. She sagged against the headboard and shakily daubed the moisture from her brow. Of course it was. Just a dream.

For over a year, she'd been free of the nightmares. The haunting dreams, reeling like slow-motion pictures in her head. Terrifying and so real—pulling her back into that small, dingy frat room.

She crunched her eyelids against the memories and yanked up the comforter to her chin. *It was only a bad dream. No one can hurt me. I'm safe.* Amber mentally chanted those thoughts over and over again.

A streak of lightning flashed outside the window, and distant thunder boomed, rattling the glass.

She sat straight up as all of her senses shot to full alert. She held her breath, listened. A creak. A pop. Another rattle.

What if she was wrong? What if she wasn't safe?

Throwing back the bedspread and sheets, she clambered out of the bed and fumbled for the light switch on the wall. She flipped up the switch and the lamp flickered on, chasing away the darkness and sending twisting shadows dancing on the pale walls and textured ceiling.

Icy chills rippled across her skin. Her gaze darted frantically around the room. What if someone was trying to get in? Even as she reminded herself that every door and window was bolted shut, she had to check again. It was a ritual she remembered well. Her voice of reason was lost in the memories. She groped the flashlight from the nightstand, ignoring the sting of cuts on her palm, and passed quickly from one room to another turning on lights and making sure everything was locked tight.

After a thorough search, she breathed relief when nothing looked out of the ordinary. As she turned out the lights, her gaze snagged on the laundry room window. The old wooden frame hung askew. Night air eerily whistled through the small gap.

She took a step closer. One of the two latches on the window was unlocked.

Someone had tampered with that window. Heart galloping, Amber tugged on the wood frame and engaged the lock, then spun on her heel, her mind reeling, grappling for a plan. Instinct told her to call the police, but what if they took too long to arrive? Maybe call a neighbor first, seek refuge—

Amber came to a screeching halt as she suddenly remembered her handyman, Charlie, had been by and cleaned her windows. He mentioned there were a couple warped window casings. He must have forgotten to latch that one.

That had to be it. She took a deep breath, rubbing her hand against the tension in her neck and scolding herself for overreacting. She'd call Charlie next week and set up a time for him to replace them.

Stalking back into her bedroom, she collapsed in the overstuffed chair by the bed, willing away the irrational fear that ripped through her like barbed wire. It was pure insanity, she knew, to be so unnerved by a dream.

Still her heart pounded to a rib-cracking beat. Over the years, she had worked hard to push past the memories. She'd done well. The nightmares had faded.

Until tonight.

Lord, if You are still near, please help me.

Amber took a steadying breath. God could protect her, she reminded herself, but at the same time she struggled to believe. Blind faith didn't seem possible anymore.

Hadn't for eleven years.

The exhaustion she'd felt earlier was gone, replaced with a restless energy, fueled by unwanted images and thoughts bouncing around in her head. She tried to tamp them down, but they wouldn't let go.

Great. Now she'd never get back to sleep. Scrubbing her hands through the thickness of her curls, she tugged her hair. She wanted to fault the chaos of the day for bringing back the nightmares and stirring the past to life, but the answer was far more complicated than that.

Patrick.

TWO

Early the next morning, Patrick arrived at his office at the police station. Plunking down in his desk chair, he slipped the elastic band from around an overstuffed file he'd picked up from the audio and video forensic unit on his way into work. With so few clues in the car-bombing case, he hoped something lurking in one of the photos might aid in his investigation.

He extracted a fistful of black-and-white crime prints. After separating them into sequence, he studied each one, starting with the blazing fire taken by first responders to the final shots of the vehicle's gray smoldering frame.

Dread settled in his gut.

As awful as bearing witness to the destruction had been, seeing the explosion and charred debris captured on film chilled him to the bone. Amateur or not, this bomb had been meant to kill. Even if forensics ruled out a terrorist link, this perpetrator definitely wanted to make a statement.

Tossing the photos on the desk, Patrick sat back and rubbed his eyes.

What kind of trouble could Amber have gotten involved in that someone would be out to kill her?

"Good morning, Wiley."

The booming voice of his supervisor ended his thoughts.

Patrick glanced up as his old friend, Department Captain Vance Peterson, walked into the room with his mouth half-full of a chicken biscuit. He was also holding a white Gus's Diner bag in his hand. "Good morning." Patrick rocked forward in his chair.

Swallowing, Vance tossed him the bag. "Here, I brought you some breakfast."

"Thanks. My growling stomach appreciates it." Patrick caught the bag, tore it open and grabbed a biscuit.

"I figured you'd be in early. I thought you might be hungry."

"You figured right." Patrick chomped right into it. All he'd consumed since he'd dropped off Amber last night was a cup of coffee, half of which was still on his desk, cold.

"So fill me in on this car-bombing case." Vance wiped his hands on a napkin.

Patrick swallowed then shrugged. "I don't have much at the moment."

"Not much?" Vance crossed his arms, his dark brows pulling tight over his eyes. "What'd the bomb squad come up with?"

"Reports are preliminary, but it looks like a homemade pressure-cooker bomb, probably propped under the car's fuel tank."

Shaking his head, Vance gave a slow whistle. "Explosives, shrapnel and gasoline. Pretty lethal combo."

Patrick jutted his chin toward the pile of photos on the desktop. "Take a look. It's amazing someone didn't get killed." He took another bite of the biscuit.

Vance moved closer and picked up the stack. He nodded slowly as he examined them, a grimace etched on his suntanned face. "And you have no clues as to who might have done this?"

"Not yet."

"What about the car owner? Or witnesses?"

Patrick finished chewing. "There was one eyewitness and he gave us a statement. He said he'd heard the blast, saw the explosion, but denies seeing anything suspicious. And interestedly enough, the owner of the vehicle was Amber Talbot. She walked away with a few bruises and lacerations but has no idea why someone would want to harm her, nor does she believe anyone was trying to."

Vance stopped, looked at him and raised his eyebrows. "Not *the* Amber Talbot from high school? Your old flame?"

Patrick nodded, hardly believing it himself. "Yeah. Definitely a surprise." Truth be told, he'd half expected to run in to her at some point now that he was back in town. However, not as part of a case he was investigating, especially one of this nature.

"I'm sure you were surprised." Vance wagged his head. "What do you think? Was this bomb meant for Amber?" He shuffled through the pictures again, studying them closer. "Or do you think this is the work of some criminal prankster?"

The question pricked the hairs on the back of Patrick's neck. He'd been up most of the night asking the same question. "I'd like to say it's random. However, my gut doesn't buy it."

Vance's eyes settled and met Patrick's. "Then Amber mustn't be fessing up to something."

Patrick paused, wondering what—if anything—Amber would be hiding. She'd always been a by-the-book kind of girl, not one who got involved in things on the wrong side of the law. Then again…

His pitched the biscuit wrapper into the trash, aware that he really didn't know Amber Talbot anymore. And he'd be foolish to believe otherwise. She'd surprised him once by walking out of his life. No telling what Amber was really like. He turned sharply in his chair and stood up. "I'll dig around and see what I can come up with."

Vance tossed the photos back on the desk. "If there's dirt, Wiley, I'm confident you'll find it."

A shudder racked between Patrick's shoulder blades. That was what he was afraid of.

Patrick gave a sharp triple knock on the crime-lab door. When a buzz sounded, he twisted the knob and let himself in. Liza Jenson, police criminologist, rose from her desk.

"Patrick Wiley." She smiled, pushing a hand through her short blond bob. "I was beginning to give up on you. I can't remember the last time you answered one of my texts with anything other than 'Sorry, working late,' or 'Too busy.'"

That was because his "I'm not interested" statement seemed to go in one ear and out the other. Patrick let her comment ride. After a couple casual dates, Liza had started dropping hints about diamond rings and dream honeymoon destinations. He'd put the brakes on that budding relationship real fast. He'd determined a long time ago he wasn't the marrying kind. Eleven years ago, to be exact. And he had a princess-cut solitaire sitting in a bank deposit box to remind him of that.

He was better off alone. And life was easier. More predictable.

"Sorry, Liza, this isn't a social call. I heard you were on this weekend and I'd like to enlist your help on a case I'm working on."

Sauntering across the tile floor, Liza worked her way toward him. "Let me guess, yesterday's car bombing on River Street."

Perceptive. He grinned. "That's the one. See what you can find out about the car owner's past. What she's been up to the past few years. Friends, hobbies, enemies. I'll do the same."

Beaming a bright smile, Liza leaned a hip against the worktable and crossed her arms. "Amber Talbot. Twenty-nine. She graduated from Trinity University, majored in psychology. She earned a graduate degree in counseling from the same school. I don't have her complete work history yet, but she recently opened Safe Harbor Counseling Center on River Street."

Impressive. Although nothing Patrick didn't already know, except for the part about Trinity University. So that was where she'd ended up after leaving College of Coastal Georgia in Brunswick. She'd traded a small state school for a private one. Patrick scratched the side of his jaw, mulling that over. "How about a husband or boyfriend, ex or otherwise?"

He held his breath, hoping his name wouldn't pop up.

Liza shook her head. "I haven't done all the checking yet, but from what I can see, she's never been married. And, right now, I've got nothing on a boyfriend."

Good. "Concentrate on the past few years and look into her financial information. Relationship issues. Consumer complaints. If something jumps out at you, let me know. I'll dig in to college and before."

"All right." Liza ran a fingernail down his arm. "Maybe we can discuss my findings over coffee or dinner."

Patrick pulled away and gave a cautious smile. "Sorry, I don't have time. Why don't you give me a call when you have something. And sooner is better." He made his way out the door.

On Monday morning, the black SUV parked several spots down was the first thing Amber noticed when she stepped out of her rental car at work. It was a rather common vehicle. Plenty roamed the streets of Savannah, but instinct told her Patrick Wiley was in the vicinity.

Patrick. She took a deep breath, ignoring the chill seeping through her, and started down River Street toward the Safe Harbor Counseling Center. Could he possibly have more questions?

Before the thought fully penetrated, the answer came. Detectives always had questions. And that was what Patrick was—the detective on the case. Nothing more.

Buoyed by that thought, Amber shouldered her messenger bag and pushed through the narrow double doors of the center. The cozy ambience wrapped around her like a warm blanket. The place was small—only had a quaint waiting area and hallway that led to three offices. And the simple decor of overstuffed seating and antique tables, framed pictures of Savannah's old harbor and a comfortable array of potted plants warmed her further.

Just being at the center made her feel better. After a long weekend of nursing her wounds and musing over Friday's bombing and Patrick Wiley, her nerves were about shot. But common sense reminded her to stop being ridiculous. Even if Patrick did show up, she would be fine.

Shedding her jacket, Amber hung it on a hook on the wall. Then she picked up a bundle of mail from a wicker basket by the front door and headed to her office, determined to have a good day as she chastised herself for her paranoia.

Two steps from her office, Amber paused when a masculine and very familiar voice sounded from behind her colleague's closed door. She bit back a gasp as her stomach did a crazy flip she couldn't explain.

Patrick.

Wrong. She wasn't fine.

The urge to put on a good face and properly welcome

him to her center quickly abated, switching instead to a desire to turn around and make a run for it.

The door to her left opened. Too late.

Tony Hill, a fellow counselor, stood next to Patrick, shaking his hand. "I appreciate your persistence in getting to the bottom of this, Detective Wiley. We sure don't need a lunatic running around blowing things up."

"I agree." Patrick turned and stepped into the hallway. "Amber." His eyes narrowed and his mouth lifted in a lop-sided grin, sending a little fluttery sensation through her midsection and making her wish he'd stick to the stoic cop face she'd seen the other night.

"Good morning." She tried for a smile, too.

"How are you? How are your injur—"

"Healing." She cut him off, holding up a bandage-free hand, aware that his gaze was washing over her.

"Glad to hear you're doing better." He smiled more broadly.

"Amber, I wasn't sure you'd be coming in today," Tony interjected, hovering in the archway. "You know Pam and I could hold down the center for a couple days."

"Thanks, Tony. I appreciate the offer, but I'm fine. Really." Amber couldn't bear to be cooped up in her house for another couple of days.

"Okay." Tony tugged on his sparse goatee. He eyed her a moment longer. "Let me know if you need anything."

"I will."

Tony shut his door and Patrick moved closer. He jerked a thumb over his shoulder, gesturing to an office door with her name engraved in bold lettering. "I have a few questions. Shall we talk in there?"

"No," Amber answered, immediately regretting the way her tone sharpened. She quickly added, "The waiting room is more comfortable." She started walking as fast as her high heels and sore knees would allow, not waiting for his reply. In the lobby, she motioned for Patrick to have a seat on the couch. Then she slipped into one of the upholstered chairs, folded her hands in her lap and tried to relax. "I'm not sure what kind of help I'll be. I don't know any more than I did on Friday."

"Actually, I have a hunch about something." Patrick ignored the sofa, pulled a chair from the wall and sat down, facing her. A little too close. She took a deep breath. "I came across something this weekend that I think may tie in to your case. And although Mr. Hill answered most of my questions, I'd like to run a couple scenarios by you."

Her stomach dropped further, but she didn't let it show on her face. Patrick was convinced the bomb was meant for her. Why wouldn't he buy into the random-crime theory like everyone else she knew? There was nothing to suggest it was anything other than that.

Patrick flipped open the folder and started shifting through the contents. Crime scene photos, detailed crime reports and other paperwork involving her case.

Amber swallowed. Maybe this was more serious than she'd thought. *No.* She tamped down the thought, reserving any speculation until there was evidence to support it.

Finally Patrick pulled a single sheet from the stack and pointed to the title with a blunt finger. "I believe this is a brochure that your center put out."

"Yes." Amber glanced at the flyer that featured the charity fund-raising dinner her counseling center was hosting. "I sent those to local businesses in the area advertising the event and requesting support." She met his gaze. "I don't understand what this has to do with the car bombing."

Patrick set the open folder on the coffee table. "Silence No More. That's the name of your fund-raiser?"

"Yes."

"Tell me about it."

"Well," Amber said with a shrug, "the fund-raiser is intended to raise money for the local women's shelter as well as promote awareness for violent assaults against women. I'm not sure if you're aware, but one in three women suffer from some sort of abuse during their lifetime. Many suffer in silence, feeling shame and guilt for something they weren't responsible for. And the challenges they live with are innumerable, like low self-esteem, depression and trust issues."

Patrick nodded. "Sounds like a worthy cause."

"Yes. It is." More than he could imagine.

Patrick scooted to the edge of his seat, arms resting on his thighs, hands clasped. "However, it brings me back to one of my earlier concerns—that the car bomb may have been planted by a revengeful abuser of one of your clients."

Drawing in a slow breath, Amber tried to detach herself from the equation and objectively consider Patrick's hypothesis. As much as it probably made sense to him, it still didn't feel right to her. She tucked a stray curl behind her ear. "Actually, the women I work with spend more time with social workers or staff at the women's shelter. Why target me?"

"Well, we have to start somewhere."

Amber fought not to shrink under Patrick's speculative stare. "Yes. That's true, but—" she held up a hand "—I was home alone all weekend. If someone wanted to hurt me—"

"It's not that simple, Amber." The grooves on either side of his mouth deepened into a frown. "This perpetrator may be lying low until the news dies down. And if he turns out to be someone from one of your clients' past, that client may very well be the next victim."

Amber's stomach lurched at the thought. She hadn't considered that. "That would be terrible."

Patrick leaned closer. So close that she caught a whiff of his cologne. Still so familiar and clean. She slid back in her seat. "Yes, it would," he concurred. "I'd like to talk to any of your clients who feel particularly threatened by someone."

Rubbing her nose, Amber sat up straighter, determined to not let him blow this incident out of proportion. "The majority of my clients feel threatened by someone. However, I have client confidentiality to consider. I can't just hand information over to you."

As a cop, Patrick should understand that.

Patrick frowned at her. Guess he didn't. "I need your help on this, Amber. I'm sure you work with a lot of vulnerable women. If any of them feel in danger, they should welcome an investigation."

Amber took a moment and considered his request, still not buying the idea, but also remembering how persistent Patrick could be. She didn't have time to argue his theory. "I guess it couldn't hurt to run the scenario by a couple of my clients. However, I don't want to start a chain of panic."

Patrick's already grim expression darkened further. "Some lunatic just blew up your car. The chain of panic has already started." He flipped the file closed and got to his feet. "Do you still have my card?"

"Yes," Amber said, standing.

"Good. Keep it with you and call me if you come up with anything."

Surely he didn't think she was being uncooperative. She simply didn't see the situation the way he did. There was no motive. No prior threats. It didn't make sense that someone was after her. Random crimes happened all the time. But apparently until Patrick exhausted his hunch, he wasn't going to consider anything else.

"All right." She nodded and offered her hand. "Thank you."

Patrick hesitated, then accepted her outstretched hand, giving it a firm shake that sent an unexpected tingle spiraling through her.

Reclaiming her hand, Amber crossed her arms tightly against her thumping chest.

"Even if you get a gut feeling, call me." Patrick turned to leave and Amber nodded, discreetly wiping her clammy palm on her skirt. Next time she'd settle for a quick wave.

She drew in a shaky breath and watched as Patrick headed out the door. He moved with the same assertive gait and athletic agility of the young man she remembered. But now he was even more fit, stronger, a capable and skilled soldier and detective.

There was a part of her that was happy he was willing to stay on her case. He could have easily passed it off to another detective. But there was also a part of her that wished he had. If the car bombing turned out to something other than a random act, the investigation would be prolonged and Patrick would be around a lot.

Both scenarios sent her heart jumping to double time.

"You okay?"

Caught up in her musings, Amber hadn't heard anyone walk in the room. She spun around and found Tony framed by the doorway, his thick eyebrows furrowed. She wondered how long he'd been there. Not that it mattered. Tony knew her story—one of the few people who did. After years of holding on to the dreadful memories, she'd recently had the courage to tell someone. It was a healing move, something she encouraged her clients to do. Talk about the hurt and pain with someone they trusted. And she trusted no one more than Tony. He had been her preceptor for her internship during her last year of college. He was a little older, nonjudgmental and wise beyond his years. With his burly physique, he looked more like a defensive lineman than a counselor, but he was good at his job. She knew that from experience.

"I'm fine." She smiled.

"You've had a rough couple of days. Remember, I'm here if you ever want to talk."

She nodded. He was so compassionate.

"By the way, this Detective Wiley, is he the same Patrick Wiley you told me about?"

And perceptive.

"Yes." She nodded.

Tony scratched his bearded chin and his left eyebrow arched. "Are you going to be okay with that?"

"I think it will be fine." She smiled, projecting a confident composure she didn't quite feel and at the same time hoping for a speedy resolution to the car-bombing case.

Her heart couldn't take too much time with Patrick Wiley.

Forty minutes later, Patrick ducked into his office and dropped into his leather swivel chair behind his desk. Grabbing the phone, he punched in the crime-lab extension. Hope for finding clues for a possible motive had fizzled about two minutes into his conversation with Amber. He couldn't figure out if she was in denial about her safety or just wasn't opening up because he was on the case.

He guessed the latter.

Maybe there was an old boyfriend she didn't want to mention or… *No.* He derailed that train of thought. Surmising never got him anywhere.

He tapped a pen against the desk as he waited for the lab to answer.

"Busy?"

At the female voice, Patrick's gaze went to the doorway. He hung up the phone. "Liza. I was just calling you."

Liza walked in the room, waving a large manila envelope. "I thought I'd drop this by and see if you were free for lunch."

"Lunch?" Patrick checked his watch, his brain racing

for a good excuse. "Actually I was going to grab something quick. I've got a ton of paperwork—"

"Then how about dinner tonight?"

He gave a quick shrug. "Racquetball with the captain."

She arched a fine brow and handed him the envelope. "Coffee after?"

More than once he had explained that he wasn't interested in a pursuing a relationship. She didn't seem to get it. He took the envelope from her. "Hey, remember, I just want to be friends."

Liza turned her head and tilted it, and one eyebrow rose even higher. "Is it a crime for friends to get together for coffee?"

She had a point. And although he wasn't crazy about the idea, he conceded, "I could meet you around seven for a quick cup."

"Perfect." She smiled. "How about Jake's Café?"

"That will work."

"Now, take a look at what I dug up on your victim, Ms. Talbot." Liza stood beside his desk and crossed her arms.

Patrick sat forward and peeled open the envelope, pulling out several pages. If nothing else, Liza was good at her job. A detailed outline stretched from Amber's college graduation to the present. Places she worked, volunteer jobs and organizations she'd interned with. Even coworkers and old roommates were mentioned. Patrick skimmed through the list. He couldn't help looking for a current or ex-boyfriend. None were listed.

"Amber Talbot has a pretty clean past," Liza said, making him refocus.

"It appears so." Patrick continued to peruse the outline.

"Currently, she's heading up a charity fund-raiser for the women's shelter."

Patrick glanced up and gave a simple nod. "Yes. She's

trying to raise awareness for violent crimes against women."

"I see you've done your homework, as well." Liza gave him a lazy smile. "The fund-raiser is in a couple weeks at the Port City Community Center in Savannah. A big crowd is expected. Amber is the keynote speaker."

"Keynote speaker?" Patrick lifted his eyes again, this time meeting hers. "She didn't mention that."

Liza shrugged. "She's one of several speakers. Maybe she didn't think it was big deal."

Patrick shoved the pages back in the envelope and clasped it shut, his brain churning through the new information. Rocking back in his chair, he crimped his lower lip between his forefinger and thumb, wondering if and why someone wouldn't want Amber to speak at the fund-raiser.

"Do you think you're on to something?" Liza asked.

"Not sure." He nodded slowly. "But I feel as though we're moving in the right direction."

In fact, his gut was reeling and he had a niggling suspicion that someone was after Amber. And whoever that was would have him to contend with him first.

At Southern Heights Gym later that day, Patrick ran around the racquetball court, breathing hard, blood pumping. He thwacked the ball coming at him, sending it screaming against the high concrete court wall.

"Dude. You don't have to kill it." Vance jerked backward, missing the shot.

When the ball arched toward him again, Patrick took another wild swing, slamming it one more time. "I'll try to ease up some," he said between breaths.

"Yeah, sure." Vance snorted, breathing heavily. He swung his racquet, sending the ball whizzing past Patrick and into the front wall. "Take that." A triumphant grin spread over his flushed face.

Maintaining his grip, Patrick turned sideways and smashed the ball again, sending it echoing around the hollow space.

"Okay. Game!" Vance jumped out of the way once more.

"What? Already?" Patrick tried to catch his breath.

"Yeah. I'm going to be nice and let you win before you bring the walls down."

"Well, thank you." Patrick peeled off his goggles and stepped off the court. He grabbed a towel from a bin. "Not often do I get three games on you."

"Don't get used to it." With his towel Vance dabbed at the sweat running down his face. "Once this case is over, we'll get back on track. Until then, I'm just going to have to make excuses not to play with you."

Taking a swig of water, Patrick almost choked on a laugh. "Maybe I'm just getting better."

"Let's hope not," Vance teased. "But seriously, Patrick, you seem pretty keyed up lately. My guess is, this car-bombing case is really getting to you. Or maybe it's seeing Amber again?"

Right on both counts. "No comment, Captain."

Vance snorted, his face redder than usual with the exertion of an hour of hard play. "You just answered my question. But like we discussed before you accepted the position, I don't want you taking the job home with you."

"Yeah, right." Patrick laughed. "Seven years as a navy SEAL. Trained to be ready. On call 24/7. Even sleep was an option."

Vance unzipped his bag and dropped his racquet in. "Patrick, I recruited you because I thought you'd be the best man for the job. I can't risk you getting burned out."

"No worries. I actually relax while I'm in the problem-solving mode."

Vance swung his towel around his neck. "Killing the

racquetball and nearly your opponent doesn't exactly indicate relaxation."

Patrick only smiled. Vance chuckled, shaking his head while he grabbed his water bottle. "Well, if that's the case, you should be pretty chilled out."

Patrick couldn't recall the last time he'd chilled out. Maybe never.

"But seriously—" the humor in Vance's voice morphed into a professional tone "—not every detective is a good fit for every case. Sometimes it's prudent to back away, let someone else have it." He paused, and Patrick fixed him with a challenging stare. "What I'm trying to say, Patrick, is that if you're not comfortable investigating Amber's case, I don't mind putting another detective on it."

"I hope you're kidding." Patrick threw his towel in a bin. "I can do my job. A lack of clues and trying to find a runaway car bomber is the stress I'm dealing with." He picked up his racquetball bag, ready to change the subject. "I need a shower."

"I'm not questioning your ability to do your job." Vance grabbed his bag and matched Patrick's steps on the way to the locker room.

"Good."

"I just remember that you and Amber didn't exactly part on the best terms."

"That's water under the bridge."

"Well, sometimes the water under the bridge is still turbulent."

Patrick didn't respond to that as they entered the locker room.

A moment passed. On a sigh, Vance added, "Patrick, if you change your mind—"

"I won't."

"You're as obstinate as ever."

"Which is why you wanted me for this job." Patrick

clapped a hand on Vance's shoulder before walking toward the showers.

"True, but…"

Patrick cranked on a shower faucet and pulled the curtain, drowning the rest of Vance's speech. He appreciated his friend, even if he did hover a bit much at times. Nonetheless, Vance's lecture held one valid point: Patrick shouldn't take his job home with him. He needed to leave work at work and learn to relax. That was one thing he promised himself that he would do when he traded military life for civilian.

Patrick scrubbed shampoo into his hair, determined to do just that. Not let his job interfere with his personal life.

Even as he firmed up those plans in his head, a dozen questions roared to life about the car bombing case. About Amber.

Then again, learning to chill out may have to wait.

THREE

Amber sat at a small iron table outside the Riverfront Bistro, and her best friend, Kim Livingston, sat across from her. Amber settled back in her chair, cradling her cup between her palms as a gentle, warm breeze rustled her hair. Street-side dining was a favorite of hers, especially on such a nice evening. A reprieve from the prolonged chilly temperatures.

If only she could shake the uneasy chill she'd been experiencing since the bombing incident and seeing Patrick again.

"You okay?"

Amber glanced up, eyeing Kim across the pastries on the table between them. "Yes. Fine."

"You don't seem *fine*." Kim set down her cup with a clink. "What's up? You're usually chatting like a magpie, but you've barely said two words since we sat down."

"Sorry, I've just been enjoying my pastry and coffee." Amber lifted her cup and took a sip. "Delicious. Hazelnut latte. My favorite."

Kim's light brows arched over her wide, inquisitive stare. "I thought you ordered caramel?"

That might explain the richer flavor. Amber took another sip. Kim was right. "Yep, definitely caramel."

Kim leaned in, brow creased. "This must be your way of dodging my question—talking about coffee flavors."

Giving a slight shrug, Amber cracked a small smile. Kim had the uncanny ability to see right through her.

"If it's the car bombing that's got you down, don't worry. It was probably just some crazy prank by an over-zealous troublemaker. In another week or two this whole thing will blow over." Hope shone in her blue eyes and her smile went wide.

Always thinking on the bright side. That was what Amber loved about Kim. "A crazy troublemaker is definitely what I'm hoping for. But, actually, I've had a lot of other things on my mind, including the upcoming fund-raiser." *And Patrick Wiley.* She spared Kim that tidbit.

She hated the way thoughts of Patrick stayed lodged in her mind. His sturdy physique, easy movements, the way his deep-set gaze swirled with questions. Which made her wonder—was the bombing incident the only thing on his mind, or were questions from eleven years ago rumbling around in his head?

Uneasiness settled heavier in her chest, followed by an immediate prick of conscience. She probably owed him some answers.

"I finally rounded up enough sponsors for the fund-raiser's silent auction." Kim's optimistic tone jerked her back to the present.

Amber blinked. "That's wonderful. Thank you so much for taking that on."

"Anything for my best friend. Besides, as an ER nurse I've seen too many abuse victims. Your efforts to bring awareness and support to those women are a blessing to me." Kim forked a cream-cheese tartlet and popped it in her mouth.

Where had Kim been during Amber's emergency room visit eleven years ago? Cold and alone. Battered and bruised after being drugged and assaulted. No one believed her story—

Stop it! Amber pushed away the dreadful memories. Buried them. She wasn't going there again.

She took another sip of coffee, trying to calm her now thumping heart.

"So what else needs to be done for the fund-raiser?"

Amber lowered her cup. "Not much...except maybe round up some volunteers to set up the reception hall and tear it down. So if you have any able-bodied friends who would like to help, let me know."

Kim paused between bites. "I'm sure I can convince a few of my coworkers to help."

"That would be wonderful. " Amber added more cream and gave her coffee a stir. "I almost forgot. I have my speech to write, too." Something she wasn't looking forward to. The topic was so close to her heart, yet it was a story she remained reluctant to share. What would be gained by her unearthing the painful memories? Her audience knew pain and guilt; what they needed was encouragement.

She picked up her cup and leaned back in the iron chair, eyeing the horse-drawn carriage trotting down the street carrying tourists on a tour of Savannah's historic district. "Isn't it nice to see spring tourists trickling in?"

At that, Kim chuckled. "As much as I'm happy to have the winter weather behind us, warmer days and tourists make for a busy ER and, if you haven't noticed, more traffic."

Amber noticed, but didn't care. She enjoyed this time of year. She sipped her coffee, watching the beautiful shires *clip-clop* past them, and as the carriage moved out of sight what came into view made her heart stop.

Patrick and his *date* seated at an outside table across

the street. Amber sucked in a mouthful of air to hold in a sigh and twisted in her chair, hoping he hadn't seen her.

Kim eyed her with raised eyebrows. "You look as though you just saw a ghost."

Worse. She set her cup on the table. "It's just someone I don't want to talk to right now."

Kim craned her neck to see around her.

"Don't look," Amber snapped, and then softened. "Sorry, I'm a little on edge."

"No kidding. So who is it that you don't want to see? The blonde or the gorgeous hunk she's with?"

Actually, Patrick with anyone was what she didn't want to see. Crazy. It had been years. Unfortunately, at the moment emotion overrode logic.

Amber picked up the laminated dessert menu on the table and used it as a fan. "The *hunk* is the detective who is investigating the car bombing."

"He's a cute one. Too bad. It looks as though he's already taken."

Amber fanned faster.

"Oh, dear."

Amber slanted a glance at Kim. "*Oh, dear*, what?"

Kim's eyes grew wide. "Detective Hunk and his friend got up from their table and are heading this way."

"Both of them?"

Kim nodded.

Amber's glance flickered to the two people across the street waiting for the light at the crosswalk. Patrick was dressed casually in jeans and a sweatshirt and stood next to a beautiful young blonde wearing slacks and a black sequined sweater. Everything about her exuded elegance and grace.

Amber had expected no less.

Still, her heart slipped.

She yanked her gaze away, hoping they were heading on a walk by the river and not coming her way. Yes, a nice evening stroll sounded like a fun couple's activity. She chastised herself for being paranoid. Of course that was what they were doing.

Concern fell away but memories swam to the surface. Of long walks along the riverfront, she and Patrick, hand in hand, talking and laughing as they glanced out across the water and admired the wave runners and colorful sailboats bobbing in the shifting seas while a light breeze rippled around them.

A simple pleasure that now Patrick probably enjoyed with someone else.

Casting an inward sigh, Amber picked up her cup and shot a forged smile at Kim, who was nibbling on a cookie and eyeing her warily.

"You sure you're okay?"

Amber nodded with more hope than conviction.

But within the next heartbeat she made a conscious decision to forget about Patrick Wiley and his personal life. No doubt a lot had changed in his life since she'd handed him back his ring.

People move on, so why shouldn't he?

Amber perked up in her seat and blew out a breath as common sense reasserted itself. Actually, she was happy for him, even if her own prospects of finding love again looked rather bleak.

"Amber."

Her heart clenched when Patrick called her name.

Shifting in her seat, she looked up as he walked over to her, his friend at his side.

"I thought that was you." He grinned widely.

Too bad he was right. "Hi, Patrick." Amber pasted on a smile and then gestured across the table. "This is a friend of mine, Kim Livingston. Kim, Patrick Wiley."

"Nice to meet you." Patrick's gaze shifted from Kim

to the woman next to him. "This is Liza Jenson. She's a police criminologist who will be helping on the case. I thought you'd like to meet her."

Even up close, Liza was lovely. Great smile, even teeth. She and Patrick made a nice couple. Amber's heart slipped further, yet she sat up straighter and held her smile, pretending that seeing him with Liza—or any woman—didn't rattle her in the least. "Nice to meet you, Liza."

Liza nodded. "Patrick and I were just talking about you."

Her smile fled. "Oh?"

"Actually we were discussing your case and trying to decide what direction to pursue next," Patrick said, curbing any speculation that his conversation with Liza involved anything about their past relationship.

The breeze intensified, blowing strands of hair against Amber's cheeks. Reaching up, she tucked them behind her ear and attempted to remain calm and put on a good face. But one look at Patrick's strong, chiseled features and her stomach did an irrational juvenile tumble. "Well, I appreciate both of your efforts to solve the case." She glanced at her watch. This little tête-à-tête was going nowhere. "Look at the time. I should get going."

"You haven't even finished your dessert." Kim shot her a questioning glance.

"Sorry. I still have things to do tonight and I'm not very hungry." At least not anymore. Amber abandoned her coffee on the table, and as she launched to her feet, her knee banged into the table leg, sending her cup crashing onto the brick pavers. Curious glances shot her way.

Amber sucked in a gasp and stumbled forward as searing pain shot through her knee and it buckled. Her ability to stand was further compromised as she tripped over her messenger bag that had slid from her shoulder.

"Amber!" Patrick called out as his strong arms wrapped around her, catching her before she hit the ground.

Patrick's solid arms kept her steady but sent her heart into palpitations. She stiffened against him, working to catch her breath as the familiar scent of his aftershave wrapped around her senses. Calm never seemed possible again.

"Are you okay?" Patrick slanted her a wary look, probably wondering why she was gasping for air like a beached trout.

She gazed into his dark eyes and nodded, her cheeks hot. "Yes, just clumsy."

Kim jumped up, grabbed a chair and scooted it forward. "Would you like to sit down?"

"No, that's okay." Amber waved off any help as her sense of equilibrium returned. She pulled out of Patrick's hold and willed her heart to slow.

She took a step; glass crunched. She glanced down and noticed the broken china at her feet. "Oh, dear, I better clean that up." She reached for some napkins, but Patrick grabbed a handful first.

"I can get it."

Amber's pulse kicked higher as she watched Patrick, who was down on one knee, pick up shattered glass and wipe up the puddle of coffee. "Thank you for doing that."

"No problem." He easily grinned.

Her chest went tight at his sense of chivalry. So attentive and helpful. When was the last time she'd met a guy like Patrick Wiley?

Never.

Suppressing a sigh, she picked up her large tote, clutched it to her side and pulled her focus back on her plans to get going.

As Patrick got to his feet, he sent her a nod. "How's your knee?"

"Better." She smiled and said, "Thank you again for taking care of the mess."

Before he could comment, she whirled around. "Good night, everyone." She left with a little parting wave, sending Kim a reassuring smile. "We'll talk soon."

Amber hiked the strap of her bag on her shoulder and headed down the sidewalk in the direction of her car, wincing at the sharp pain in her knee and doing her best to avoid limping while hoping her sutures stayed intact.

As she made a turn onto Mulberry Street, she heard someone behind her. She hated feeling paranoid, but the sound of heavy boots clapping against the pavement made her pulse race. She quickened her gait, her eyes pointed forward.

The boot steps accelerated, moving closer, then came up directly behind her. She was suddenly struck with an eleven-year-old memory. Her pursuer's thudding footsteps the night she was attacked. So quickly he came at her and once he grabbed her—

A hand caught her arm and panic exploded in her chest. As a silent scream ballooned in her throat, she wheeled around, adrenaline surging…and saw Patrick. Catching her breath and willing her heart to slow, she felt equal parts disappointment and relief.

"Amber, what happened back there?"

"Back at the café?" She pulled away and started walking again, trying to regulate her breathing. "Do you mean why I left?"

Patrick kept pace with her. "You didn't just leave. You took off like a scared jackrabbit."

So she had been that obvious? Amber didn't slow down, but cast a sidelong glance his way. "I didn't mean to be rude. I just have a lot on my mind." *Patrick Wiley included.*

"I understand that you don't like to dwell on what happened, but the truth is, a bomb blew up your car and we need to figure out who did it."

Even on his night off, didn't this man rest? "I understand your need to investigate the crime, Patrick. I just didn't expect to see you when you're off duty."

Patrick continued walking beside her. "Well, I thought you'd like to meet Liza, since she's working on the case with me."

"I don't want to seem unappreciative. I'm just holding out hope that this whole ordeal will blow over soon."

"That's all of our wishes. But in the meantime, we need to work together."

Obviously an easy feat for him, but for her... Well, not so easy.

Amber stopped at the street corner, waiting for the light to change green. Eyes forward, heart thumping, flustered that Patrick stood so close.

She could feel the intensity of his gaze and the tension sizzling like electricity between them.

"I feel as if we're missing something," Patrick said after a moment. "Some vital component to this crime that's right under our noses. Is there anything you need to tell me?"

Guilt swamped her. She felt blood rush to her cheeks, probably turning them the color of the red glowing traffic light. She had a million things to tell him. But not here. Not now. And not about the bombing incident. She sent him a glance and fought not to squirm under his speculative gaze.

"Patrick, honestly, the whole bombing thing baffles me as much as it does you. If that changes, I promise to call."

After a moment's hesitation, he nodded, his brow furrowed. "Okay. Let me walk you to your car."

"No need. I'm just in the parking garage across the street." The light changed. "Have a good night." With a wave, she broke into a jog, refusing to look back.

A half hour later, Amber pulled into her driveway as

the night sky twinkled to life. Five steps took her to her covered front porch. As she plunged the key into the lock, her mind was already plotting her evening. Number one on her list: narrow down the fund-raiser's agenda and finish working on the speech she'd started.

She blew out a breath. Good thing she'd left the café when she did.

Once inside, she flipped on the hall lights and locked the dead bolt.

Creak.

The sound split the silence, sending an icy tendril of fear skipping up her spine. Amber froze. Fisting her ring of keys, she held her breath, cocked her head to listen, hoping it was nothing. Ten…twenty seconds, then a floorboard creaked again.

A footstep!

Nerves sputtering, Amber whirled around as her brain maniacally chanted, *Get out of here!*

The lights flickered a split second before the power went out, thrusting her in total darkness.

The rush of blood pounding in her ears merged with the thud of approaching footsteps. Frantically, she grabbed for the dead bolt. As she untwisted the lock, a steely, gloved hand grabbed on to her wrist.

"You're not going anywhere!" the man barked as he whipped her around and jerked her hard against his muscular chest.

The bloodcurdling scream scuttling up her windpipe quickly abated when a gloved hand clamped over her mouth.

"Amber, it has been a long time," he whispered, his voice gravelly, distorted. He tightened his hold on her.

She desperately clawed at her memory, trying to recognize the gruff voice. Nothing registered.

"Yes, long enough, dear, for you to forget. And if you had been smart, you would have."

Forget what? Her attempt to make sense of the man's words was interrupted by his husky growl in her ear. "Eleven years of silence. Now you're an advocate for assault victims. Do you really think you can make atonement for past regrets?"

Panic seized Amber as clarity seeped into her brain. Her assailant was back. He knew she was speaking at the Silence No More fund-raiser and feared her story would go public. Immediately, she began to fight—she kicked out her legs, and her body bucked against his. She screamed into his hand, but it was cut off, coming out as a squeak.

Muscled arms tightened around her, crushing her lungs, stopping air flow. "Remember, Amber, some secrets are best taken to the grave." His garbled whisper was hot and fast on her neck.

As her lungs struggled for a breath, she clawed at the man's hand hard enough that he slackened his grip from her mouth. She then spluttered, "I don't even know who you are."

His harsh laugh jarred her eardrums.

He didn't believe her. A jolt of disbelief morphed into terror, catapulting her back to a dark and cold frat house bedroom. This man was here to kill her.

Fear suddenly dissolved into rage. No way was she going to let him take her life.

From deep inside her, survival instincts kicked into gear. Biting her lip, she kicked the heel of her shoe into his shin, then jerked back her head so it connected with his jaw.

"You little—" His wail pierced the air.

With dreadful memories spurring her on, Amber broke away. She spun around, lifted the pepper spray on her key chain and sprayed the man in the face.

He stumbled back, hitting the wall with a thud.

Gasping and dizzy, Amber burst out the front door and into the street.

Patrick climbed into his SUV, and before he even started the vehicle a shrill ping on his cell phone announced the arrival of a new text message. He grabbed his handset from the clip on his belt and read the text from Liza.

Enjoyed tonight. Let's do it again soon.

"Let's not." Patrick shook his head. It was impossible to just be friends with the woman. He clicked off the phone and tossed it on the seat beside him.

Another ping.

Really. Ignoring the pesky tone, Patrick plunged the key into the ignition and fired up the powerful V8.

A third ping.

"Relentless woman." Debating whether to silence it, he grabbed the cell phone and glanced at the message. It wasn't from Liza. It was Amber.

The police are swarming my house. Someone had broken in and was waiting for me when I got home. Apparently the bomb was meant for me after all.

Frustration exploded in Patrick's chest. Yanking the gearshift into Reverse, he peeled out of the parking lot and headed in the direction of Amber's house. This was exactly what he'd been afraid of.

He scrolled through the contacts on his phone, punched on Amber's name.

"Come on. Come on." Patrick turned down a side street, taking a shortcut, waiting for her to answer.

Finally, "Hello."

"Amber?"

"No, this is Kim, a friend—"

"Kim, this is Patrick Wiley. I met you this evening."

"The detective?"

"Yes. Where's Amber?"

"She's talking to some of the officers here. Don't worry, she's okay."

Thank You, God. "I'll be right there."

Someone cut in front of him and he leaned on the horn, the thrum of blood pounding in his ears. Ten minutes later he slammed on his brakes and nosed his SUV in between two patrol cars outside Amber's bungalow.

As soon as his boots hit the pavement, he saw her. Surrounded by a handful of patrol officers, she stood there with her arms locked around her waist, her face expressionless beneath the glow of police flashlights.

Patrick approached the small group. His jaw tightened along with his fist when he thought about someone trying to harm her. Even after eleven years, he felt a need to protect her.

"What do you know, Gil?" Patrick directed his question at one of the officers.

"It seems somebody broke into Miss Talbot's house. Got in through the laundry room window. He was waiting for her when she got home." He nodded toward Amber. "Fortunately, she got away without being hurt."

Patrick's gaze bounced to Amber. "Did you get a look at him?"

Amber shook her head. "No, the lights were off and it was too dark."

"So her attacker got away?" Patrick asked the officer.

Gil removed his hat, scratched at his sparse hairline. "Yes, sir. Once Miss Talbot got away from him, the crook didn't hang around. But we've got the forensics team working on fingerprints."

"Good." Although Patrick wouldn't hold his breath. Criminals today were savvy. Too many seasons of *CSI*. Whoever was after Amber meant business and wouldn't be careless.

"And Roberts and his team have their dogs out scouring the area," Gil added.

Patrick nodded. "Have you gotten a complete statement from Miss Talbot?"

"Yes, sir, we did."

"Then I'll take it from here. Thanks for your work, guys."

The group started to disperse, leaving Amber standing beside him.

"How are you doing?" He draped his arm around her shoulder, breaking his own rule on getting personal with victims. But he had to admit, for the second time in one day, it felt good having Amber in his hold.

Amber shuddered slightly beneath his touch, but didn't pull away. "I've had better evenings."

He was experiencing the same feeling. "Do you have a new revelation on why someone would want to hurt you?"

After an endless moment, Amber took a deep, quavering breath and nodded weakly. "Yes."

Patrick raised a brow. Now they were getting somewhere.

FOUR

A corner booth at the Riverside Café was the most private place Amber could think of to talk to Patrick. She no longer felt safe in her home and didn't feel comfortable going to the police department—Patrick's stomping ground. The private matter she had to discuss with him was better said in a neutral environment, over a cup of coffee.

That was if there even was a good place.

Thankfully, Patrick agreed to hold any questions until after they arrived.

Amber dropped her bag on the booth seat and scooted in beside it. Patrick settled into the seat across the table from her, and his gaze, full of questions, met hers. He was waiting for her to tie up the loose ends of the case. She inhaled slowly to calm her nerves.

Patrick propped both elbows on the table, clasped his hands. "So you think you know who your attacker is?"

"Yes and no." She adjusted herself in her seat, the vinyl squeaking beneath her, as she gave a slight shrug.

He raised his eyebrows. "You've lost me already."

Not a surprise. The breath she'd just sucked in sputtered out in a rush, snarling her nerves again. She was grateful that the waitress arrived to take their orders.

"You guys know what you want?"

"Amber." Patrick gestured to her.

Forgoing her usual favorite, a decaf latte, she ordered a nice, strong cup of black brew. Somehow she felt as though she'd need it.

"I'll take the same." Patrick nodded at the waitress, then turned his gaze back on Amber. "Why don't you start at the beginning."

A wave of emotion burned in Amber's eyes. *The beginning.* He made it sound so simple. She took a slow breath, feeling the heat of his gaze on her, but finding it difficult to meet the dark cop stare. Persistent. Unwavering. No doubt, he was successful in the art of interrogation for suspects and criminals alike. He'd always had a knack for being perceptive. It was impossible to keep things from him.

That was why she couldn't have stuck around after being attacked at the frat party. And here she was eleven years later having to explain that to him.

She placed a finger to her temple and rubbed where a dull pain started to thump.

"Amber." By the coaxing in his voice it was evident he was waiting for answers. Answers he deserved. Not because he was the detective on her case, but because he was the man she used to love.

Amber met his gaze, trying to stay calm and downplay the agony roiling inside her. "The man who attacked me tonight mentioned something that sent me back eleven years."

"Eleven years?" Patrick's jaw visibly tightened, telling her she'd hit a nerve. "And what would that be?"

Amber breathed deep again, before she went on, "He said some secrets are best taken to the grave."

"Secrets?" Patrick leaned in, an edge of curiosity in his tone. "What kind of secrets?"

"A very difficult secret…" Her voice dropped several octaves as a lump formed in her throat. She swallowed it back.

A little pool of silence engulfed the booth. She was trying to keep it together and best phrase her thoughts without stirring up more emotion between her and Patrick. But as she looked back into her past, neither the horror of her attack nor the shame she'd suffered since seemed good enough reason for her decision to keep what had happened that night from him. Not even her concern over how he would react when he heard the story.

She looked up and Patrick's gaze linked with hers, causing her to sit up straighter and stiffen her spine. It was time to get this over with. She opened her mouth, then closed it as the waitress plunked their coffee down on the table.

"Cream or sugar?"

"No," they both said in unison.

"Thank you, though," Amber added.

"No problem." The waitress spun away, and Amber picked up her coffee, reaching for courage that still eluded her.

"Please continue." Patrick's coffee sat untouched, steam rising from the cup. He sat back in the booth and folded his arms.

A searing sensation washed over her eyes. She blinked, keeping the tears at bay, wishing she could do the same with the darkened memories. But there was no going back. "Patrick, before I get into this, I want you to know that you were the last person I ever wanted to hurt."

The perplexed look was back.

Guilt ate at her. This was Patrick's investigation. And here she was, about to put a personal spin on the case.

Patrick's brows knit as he narrowed his gaze. "I'm not sure what's going on or how it ties into your case, but I'm getting vibes that what you're trying to tell me is that you broke our engagement for another guy."

His assumption hit her like a blow to the stomach. "No," she said automatically, meeting his accusatory stare. "I can't believe you'd even consider that." Nothing could be further from the truth.

"Well, I can't lie and say that scenario hadn't crossed my mind in the past," Patrick said, his mouth compressing to a tight, razor-thin line.

Swallowing the sour taste in her throat, Amber willed herself not to cry. Patrick was frustrated and angry. And he had every right to be.

This confession was even more difficult than she envisioned.

Her mouth suddenly dry, she picked up her coffee and took a sip.

Patrick felt his patience waning. If Amber hadn't left him for another guy, what else would she be hiding that could be worse than that? He searched her anguished expression for answers to years of pent-up questions.

He came up with nothing. Except… A horrifying thought took hold as his detective instincts kicked in, replacing any speculation and doubt. Suddenly, the pieces started to meld together. Their abrupt breakup. The way she'd walked out of his life with barely a civil goodbye.

Pressure built in his chest until he could barely breathe around it. The hurt and rejection that gripped him eleven years ago had kept him from seeing the truth.

Until now.

Oh, Lord, no. He hoped his assumption was wrong, but…

"Amber, did somebody hurt you?" His voice pulsed low. "Did they—"

She nodded quickly, sparing him from having to finish the question. Her lips parted just enough to inhale a breath of air. No words came forth.

"Amber."

She swallowed quickly, tried again. "I set myself up,

Patrick." Her lips compressed when her voice wavered some. "You warned me more than once not to get sucked into the social scene at college. To stay away from the parties."

For good reason. A sheltered girl reeking of innocence had no business hanging out in those circles. Intoxicated partygoers and drug seekers who lived for the thrill of the moment. He took a deep breath of his own. "You always looked for good in everyone. Trusted easily."

"Too easily." Amber shook her head. "Every weekend my roommates invited me to attend a party with them. And the one time I gave in…" She closed her eyes, took a moment before continuing. "I ended up getting drugged, assaulted and dumped in an alley."

Patrick's lower jaw went slack. He was speechless, incensed. Who would have done such a terrible thing? "When you say *assaulted*, Amber, was it a physical assault or se—"

"Fortunately, no," Amber interjected sharply, holding her hand to her chest as if she was trying to keep her heart from jumping out. "He was interrupted before it got that far."

Patrick thanked God for that. Although the strain in Amber's voice told him the creep had done plenty of damage. A muscle angrily pulsed in his jaw. He couldn't wait to bring her attacker to justice. "Amber, who did this to you?"

She gave a quick shrug, wiping the tears from her eyes with a napkin. "That's the crazy part. I don't know."

"Don't know? Or don't remember?"

"I don't know…exactly."

"But you suspect someone?"

A gloominess crept into Amber's eyes as she nodded weakly.

Patrick gave her a moment, silently praying for God's

strength to be with her. He knew this had to be difficult for her to talk about.

"When I first arrived at the party three guys I knew from high school paid a lot of attention to me." Amber sighed, absently running a hand through her dark curls. "At first we were just reminiscing, and then they asked about you. How you were enjoying UGA and how your track season went. They even knew you were in Europe doing a training clinic. I remember thinking how much they'd grown up. They were so jealous of you in high school."

"These guys... Were they by any chance Carl Shaw, Bruce Austin and Randall Becker?"

She hesitated, then nodded. "Yes."

Patrick's heart tripped wildly in his chest. If one of those guys had touched her... He gritted his teeth, forced himself to stay calm and not start throwing darts until he had the facts. Still, he recalled his rivals well, and those memories weren't fond. "What about your roommate? The girl you attended the party with?"

"Once we got there everyone scattered. The house was packed with people. Everyone was drinking. It was hot and stuffy. Someone offered me a bottle of water."

Patrick shook his head. He knew where this was going.

"It tasted like regular water." She broke off, breathing deep. "It was cold, refreshing at first, then I started feeling woozy. Everything started moving in slow motion. That's when Carl's, Bruce's and Randy's demeanors started to change. They went from being friendly to taunting me about you. Asking me things like 'Does Boy Wonder, the gold-medal dreamer, know he's dating a party girl?'"

She stopped, blotted her eyes again with the crumpled napkins. Her silence told him what he needed to know. His throat went tight as a picture began to form in his mind of what she'd gone through—frightened and alone, unable to fend off her attacker. Heat swarmed his body.

"I was so sick," she finally squeaked out. "So disoriented. Somehow, I ended up in one of the fraternity bedrooms."

"Alone?"

"No." She sighed, her voice hollow. "It was dark. Cold. Someone was laughing. Deep. Sinister. He kept asking the question, 'Where is Boy Wonder now? Now who's going to save you?' I remember panicking, trying to get to the door, but he caught me, slammed me against the wall. He threatened to kill me if I said a word."

Patrick swallowed, fury building in his chest as she went on.

"Thankfully a few minutes later someone pounded on the door, screaming that a fight had broken out and police had been called. The last thing I remember is a hand clamped over my mouth and the prick of a needle in my arm. When I woke up I was in an ambulance on my way to the hospital. My clothes were torn, my body battered and bruised."

"Did you tell anyone what happened?

She nodded. "I informed the paramedic, the nurse, even the doctor. I was pretty groggy and disoriented. I'm sure they thought I had just been out partying. I was found in an alley behind a bar in the low-rent side of town after the manager called 9-1-1, with the needle still in my arm."

"They left the needle in your arm?" The very idea turned Patrick's gut. They'd been trying to make her look like a strung-out addict who'd overdosed.

"A urine screen found fentanyl in my system."

A very potent opiate. Patrick took a deep breath. "So no one believed your story?"

Shaking her head, Amber brushed a wisp of hair from her face. "Once I was stable, I was given a pamphlet on the risks of IV drug use and the address of a local rehab facility."

Well, that answered that. Patrick rubbed the cords of tension at the back of his neck. A lot of college-aged partiers used opiates for their euphoric effect, and ER workers probably saw their share of unintentional overdoses, but still it burned his gut that they'd disregarded Amber's story.

But what hurt even more, she hadn't told him.

He hauled in a deep breath. "I know you went through a terrible experience. But I don't understand why you kept it from me."

The corners of Amber's mouth quivered into a grimace. "I couldn't." Her tone was anguished.

The earth felt as if it shifted beneath him. "You couldn't?"

Shaking her head with a sigh, Amber lowered her gaze to her coffee and slowly ran her finger along the handle of her cup. "I was so broken, Patrick. Embarrassed, tired, scared. I had hoped by the time you got back from Europe, I could have put what happened behind me. But..." Amber kept trailing the rim of the cup, still carefully averting her gaze. "The closer it came to your returning home, the more I realized it would be impossible for me to keep a secret from you."

Well, she'd done a pretty good job of that for the past eleven years. Then the truth hit him, pounding at his temple with the force of a sledgehammer.

"You broke up with me because you thought I would blame you?"

Disappointment sparked bright in her gaze. "No, I'd never think that."

"Then what?" He worked to keep his voice even in spite of the boulder sitting in the pit of his stomach.

"It's just that..." Amber's voice cracked as her eyes clung to his. "You would have muscled every guy who attended the party until you found out who my attacker was. And once you found him..." She paused, drew in a shaky breath. "Patrick, none of those guys would have had a chance against you. A charge of assault and battery, regardless of the reason, would have jeopardized your college scholarship and your athletic dreams."

Cold sweat erupted on his skin. She'd tried to protect him. He wanted to discount her words, to be furious, but her concerns held some validity. He'd been a star athlete out to conquer the world. Cocky, impulsive and known for a quick temper. Nobody messed with him.

Foolish bravado. He shook his head. And for what?

False hope in a dream he'd never realized. After years of hard work and training, impressing his coaches and trying to stay on top of his competition, all it had taken was a broken leg to knock him out of the US track-and-field trials.

In a flash the notoriety had vanished, as had his chance of winning a gold medal.

A sigh crawled up his throat, but he swallowed it back. It'd been a lesson in futility, he'd decided. And stupidity.

"Amber, I'm sorry." That was all he could say.

Her chin trembled, but she tempered it quickly and breathed deeply, seeming to pull strength from the air. "It's just part of the past." She nodded, a gritty resolve in her eyes. Something she'd accepted and moved on.

All the same, something in that emerald gaze contradicted that opinion. In his heart he knew she'd meant to protect him, but she had hurt both of them and shaken her faith in the process.

An hour later and Amber's shocking revelation still haunted Patrick's thoughts. He was beyond frustrated, his thinking disjointed, his mind numb and swirling, blaming, stinging.

Amber had gone through unspeakable trauma. As a cop and an elite military soldier, he didn't need an imagination to know how ruthless some people could be. What he had a hard time getting his mind around was that she'd chosen to suffer through it herself.

Anger built in his chest, for himself and anyone else that kept what happened from him—even Amber.

Pent-up emotions and dozens more spiked through him with savage force. Gritting his teeth, he swung his SUV out of Kim's driveway. Amber was safe at her friend's house for the night. Cell phone in reach, security system on, doors locked tight.

He was wired. What he hadn't understood eleven years ago, he was still trying to understand now. Why had Amber just walked away? He wanted to stay mad, disappointed, but how could he? She gave up on their dreams of a life together...to protect him.

Protect me! Patrick slammed his hand against the steering wheel. Every muscle tensed, every fiber hummed. He wouldn't have faulted her for attending the party. He'd made plenty of foolish mistakes himself.

His own sense of failure cut him to the quick. If only she'd trusted him enough, maybe she would have come to him.

He wanted to believe he would have kept a level head. Supported her. Let the police do their job. Not do something as impulsive as break down doors in search of her attacker.

But...

He knew better than that.

Tightening his fingers on the steering wheel, he shook his head.

Now that he worked as a law enforcement officer, he loathed people who interfered with his investigations. Knowing the way he was back then, he would have made a few enemies, for sure.

Patrick gritted his teeth, then released the breath he'd been holding.

Thankfully those days were behind him.

Although, too little too late.

Patrick slowed at the blinking lights of an intersection before proceeding through.

When Amber walked out of his life, she'd taken part of his heart with her. For years he couldn't get her out of his head, couldn't stop wondering how she was doing. Stubbornness had kept him from picking up the phone, especially when his dreams of becoming a champion runner had begun to unravel.

One more reason to wallow in misery.

Nope, he hadn't handled disappointment well, so how could he fault Amber for handling the pain in her life the way she had? He'd nearly given up himself when his dreams had crashed and burned. What had finally got him straight was a kick in the pants from his boot-camp training officer, who taught him to persevere and thrive on adversity. To be a man.

As a result he got stronger. Less impulsive and hopefully wiser.

He firmly rubbed at his right temple, where a definite headache started to form, then stopped short as a thought barreled into his brain. If he'd gained any wisdom over the years, what was he thinking, leaving Amber alone tonight?

A block from his condo, Patrick turned into the first fast-food restaurant he saw open. Almost midnight, but the odds of a good night's sleep were slim to none. He was agitated and still buzzed from adrenaline the evening with Amber had wrought. As long as he was awake he might as well get in a little surveillance. A cup of coffee and burger should hold him until morning.

FIVE

More relaxed in her sweatpants and T-shirt, Amber accepted a cup of brewed tea from Kim and sank onto the soft cushions of her friend's blue tweed sofa. Propping her sore legs on the coffee table, she tried to forget the past few hours.

At least for tonight.

Patrick was already running a check on the guys from high school, and tomorrow they'd meet to further discuss her short list of suspects. After a good night's sleep. Hopefully by then her mind would be ready.

And her emotions.

Dredging up the past would be difficult. Even worse, knowing that one of those suspects was out to kill her made her skin crawl. And as much as she appreciated Patrick's diligence to keep her safe, having him around was going to be uncomfortable for both of them.

Swallowing a sigh, she raised her teacup and gently blew on the steamy vapors.

"I know it's not safe for you to go back home for a while, and I want you to know that you're welcome to stay with me as long as you'd like," Kim said, walking into the room.

Amber gave her a small smile. "I can't thank you enough." The last thing she wanted was to pull her friend into her mess. But between Patrick's prodding and Kim's insistence that she stay with her instead of at a local hotel, Amber's choice was made. Since her parents were a world away helping with her brother's ministry in Chile, she was truly thankful for a friend like Kim.

"So, do you have any gut feeling about who this lunatic is?" Kim settled into one of the overstuffed armchairs.

Tension pulled at Amber's shoulders. Though her friend had asked a good question, Amber didn't have the mental energy to go through the story again. "Nothing conclusive."

"But you have some idea, at least a direction to go in. Right?" A troubled look crept across Kim's face as she narrowed her blue eyes.

Amber nodded. "Yes. We definitely have more of a direction than before. One little blessing amid the chaos, I suppose." Tell that to the knot in her stomach, she thought.

"Patrick being the detective on the case is another added bonus." A goofy grin spread across Kim's face, and her gaze turned downright mischievous. "I can't believe you ever let that guy go."

Now Amber regretted telling Kim she'd once been engaged to Patrick. It'd been a lifetime ago, but now her romance-loving friend would never let her forget it. "Things didn't work out for us, although I'm sure he's a fine detective." However, the biggest issue with him being on her case was spending more time with him. Patrick could be dangerous. Her heart kicked at the reminder.

"And a hunk of a man."

Amber took a sip of tea and shrugged. "One that apparently has a cute little blonde in his life." *Ouch.* Just saying that hurt.

"Maybe not," Kim quipped. "I didn't see a ring on her finger."

Amber tucked a stray curl behind her ear and settled

back against the cushions. "Hardly a reason to discount a relationship."

Kim smiled and reached across the coffee table to refill her teacup. "Just for the sake of discussion, let's assume he's not in a relationship."

Amber curled her hands around her cup, the warmth seeping through. No way would she allow her mind to even entertain that thought. "Well, maybe," Amber teased, "I could try to fix you up with him."

Kim roared and protested. "I'm not the one I was aiming to fix him up with."

Amber needed to end this conversation before her nerves frayed any further. "Kim, I'm pretty exhausted and it's really late."

Kim nodded and gave her a knowing smile. "I know you've had a rough day. I have the guest room set up for you."

Setting down her cup, Amber got up from the couch. She was exhausted.

Hours later, after a restless slumber, she looked at the glowing red numbers on the bedside clock. Nearly 3:00 a.m. Thanks to memories mingling with new fears, and caffeine overload, she was no closer to sleep than she'd been when she crawled into bed at midnight.

She pulled a pillow over her head and crimped her eyes shut, willing herself to sleep.

Minutes passed. Nothing.

With a tired groan, she tossed the pillow aside and wrenched back the covers. Wearing the oversize nightshirt she'd borrowed from Kim, she got out of bed and crept down the darkened hallway, her bare feet squeaking against the wood floors. A cold drink was what she needed.

She opened the refrigerator and grabbed a bottle of water. Taking a swig, she padded to the bay window facing the street, lifted one slat of the blind and gazed out. A pale sliver of moon floated against a star-spangled sky. Peaceful and quiet.

Suddenly, her heart kicked with an overwhelming awareness that nearly stole her breath. An awareness that reminded her that God had created this beauty and more. He could keep her safe.

Closing her eyes, she breathed deep to fill her lungs. For a long moment she pondered that truth, waiting for peace to surround her. But niggling fears and doubt kept that from happening.

On a sigh, she tugged on the pull cord and lifted the blinds this time. The street was quiet, bathed in the soft orange glow of the historic ornamental streetlamps. She leaned in, casting her gaze around, slowly searching the yard and the street, watching for anything suspicious.

Nothing looked out of the ordinary. No lurking figures. No movement at all. However, who knew what lingered beyond the glow of the streetlamps? It was too dark to tell if anyone might be out there.

Stalking. Waiting.

Her nerves fluttered and she turned to glance out the window again. Taking careful assessment of the area, her gaze stalled on the neighbor's house across the street. The wide front porch was lit, with a vehicle parked along the curb. Everything inside her froze.

Patrick's truck.

The SUV resonated of commitment and security. Still, it was not enough to immediately dampen her concerns, the panic of the day still fresh in her mind.

She stood there a moment longer, taking a long pull of water as if to wash away her fears. Cleanse the memories that she could no longer hide.

"Patrick," she muttered. A wave of gratitude swelled up to replace the melancholy. Regardless of past regrets, he was trying to protect her. She closed her eyes, breathed deep and lifted a prayer of gratefulness. Maybe God was protecting her.

At the rhythmic *tap, tap, tap* on the window, Patrick woke up instantly, alert and ready as his years as a navy SEAL had trained him. Squinting against the sun blaring through the windshield, he pulled himself up in the driver's seat of his SUV. The last thing he remembered was dawn breaking.

"Good morning, Patrick."

Turning, he met Amber's eyes through the side window, and a warm rush of pleasure overrode the surprise. She smiled, cutting cute little dimples into her cheeks.

Patrick lowered the window. A brush of cool air mixed with Amber's sweet perfume oozed through the opening. This was the first time since the investigation started that she actually appeared happy to see him. "Well, good morning, Amber." He returned the smile.

"Sorry to wake you."

"No problem. I dozed off, I guess." He pulled himself up straighter in the seat. He never really slept. At least not deeply.

"I brought you some coffee." She handed him an insulated mug through the open window. The rich aroma tugged at his senses. Caffeine—exactly what he needed.

"Thank you."

"You're welcome." Amber's edgy smile and the blush creeping into her face as she went on warmed his heart. "I noticed you didn't stray far last night."

"Yeah, well, it's just part of the job."

Her shapely brows drew together, causing her eyes to narrow, and Patrick immediately wished the words back. *Just part of the job...* It sounded...well, as though he was just doing his job. Way too impersonal.

She gave a small shrug. "Still, I appreciate it."

In reality, it was more than that. He wanted her safe and wasn't about to trust anyone else with that job. He opened his mouth to clarify, but Amber took over.

"I brought you this." She pulled a single sheet of paper from her bag and handed it to him. "It's the list of people I remember seeing at the frat party. Most are old high school classmates."

Patrick stepped out of the SUV and took the list from her, placing his drink on the hood. "We'll start making calls today and get a statement from everybody. Who knows, maybe one of them will recall something that will help us."

"I hope so."

Patrick leaned against the door and studied the list, trying to put a face to the names he recognized. Eleven years was a long time, and he had a hard time recalling some of his classmates. He wondered how many would remember attending the fraternity party. Or even Amber Talbot. He didn't pin much hope on any grand discoveries, but it never hurt to try.

Instinct told him to start his investigation with Carl, Bruce and Randall. He made that his number one priority for the day.

It chilled him to think that the man who'd attacked Amber and had drugged her and left her in an alley to die had been running free for the past eleven years. This criminal should have been brought to justice years ago.

Who knows, maybe things would have worked out differently between him and Amber? Maybe—

Whoa, Wiley... Leave it alone.

Patrick straightened up to his full six-foot-two height, gaining control of his runaway emotions. They had no business in this investigation. He folded the paper and stowed it in his pocket.

Everything happens for a reason, he reminded himself. Looking back, the odds had been against them from the get-go. Youth, immaturity and the fact that they'd attended separate colleges on the opposite sides of the state were hardly conducive to a lasting romance.

The sharp trill of his cell phone cut short his thoughts. He pulled it from his belt holster and held it to his ear. "Wiley here."

"Good morning, Patrick." Liza's sultry voice drifted over the phone line. "I hope I didn't wake you."

"No. I'm awake. What do you know?" Patrick glanced at his watch, wondering what time it was. Seven-twenty. He had napped some.

"Not even a good-morning?" Liza sighed.

"Sorry. Good morning, Liza." Patrick's gaze drifted back to Amber…to her sparkling green eyes. Eyes that met his and widened. He held up a finger and mouthed, *I'll be done in a minute.* He didn't want to take a chance of her scooting away.

She nodded and he smiled, noticing how nice she looked dressed in stylish jeans, a purple silk blouse and high-heel sandals. Her hair was pulled back in some delicate twist, except for a few unruly curls ruffling in the breeze.

Patrick swallowed, frustrated from even noticing her appearance.

"I did a little investigative search on the three names you sent last night." Liza's words brought his thoughts back to the job he needed to do.

"What did you come up with?"

"For one, Bruce Austin was a marine."

"A marine? Interesting."

"Don't get too excited. He was killed in Iraq five years ago."

Patrick's heart sank a little. He and Bruce had never seen eye to eye on much. All through school they'd been fierce competitors in sports and academics. But Patrick felt a wash of sadness for anyone who had died for his country and was so young.

"Too bad about Bruce." There was now one less suspect to contend with. "What about the other two?"

"Carl Shaw is employed by the Chatham County public school system. He works as a gym teacher and a coach for Cavalier High School."

His and Amber's alma mater. "Gym teacher and coach?" Patrick crossed one ankle over the other. "Well, if Carl's the culprit, I'm sure he wouldn't want a story about drugging and assaulting a woman to come out, not to mention attempted murder. What about Randall Becker?"

"Mr. Becker is the owner and manager of Coastal Karate School."

Patrick gave a slow whistle. "Think of all those kids on his roster. He has a ton to lose also if rumors start flying."

As he spoke, Amber stood ramrod straight, arms clasped tightly over her chest. Face blank, she stared at him. He sent her a tentative smile. She didn't respond.

"That's as much as I have so far. I thought you'd find it interesting."

"I do. Thank you, Liza. I have a few more names I'll be sending over to you today."

"Or you can drop by with them. I'll be here all day."

Patrick changed the phone to the other ear, suddenly self-conscious about the direction of the conversation with Amber standing in such close vicinity. Crazy. He had no intention of getting romantically involved with either woman. Still…

He cleared his throat. "I'll email you the list. I have a lot going on today."

"All right." Liza sighed. "I'll call if I come up with anything else."

"I'd appreciate that."

Patrick clicked off his phone, his eyes still on Amber. A succession of emotions flitted across her face from a touch of chagrin to annoyance.

"You told Liza what happened to me?" Her voice remained soft, but he could hear the hurt in her tone.

Patrick froze, stunned for a moment as he stared at her. Did she expect him to keep the information to himself? "Amber, everything that happened to you at the frat party is pertinent to this case. And everyone on the investigative team is privy to the data collected."

"Of course. That makes perfect sense." Amber shrugged, looking close to tears but trying to be nonchalant. "I just hadn't considered who would need to know."

Patrick took a step toward her. "Don't think for a moment that I take what happened to you lightly. Believe me, I want whoever did this to you found and brought to justice."

She nodded, her lashes lowering and shielding whatever emotion was in her eyes. "It's all new to me," she explained. "Talking about a part of my life I tried so hard to forget. Although I understand why it's necessary."

Her accepting words were completely at odds with the catch in her voice.

Sadness seized his chest like a giant fist clenching on to his heart when he thought about how long she'd kept this bottled up. Accepting the guilt for a crime in which she was the victim.

He knew it was a bad idea, but with her standing there, endeavoring to be strong, the need to comfort her catapulted to a new level. Patrick couldn't keep himself from taking her in his arms. "I know this is difficult for you," he whispered against the top of her head, "but please trust me. I'm going to walk with you through this and keep you safe."

Nodding against his chest, she emitted a small sob. And then gingerly, she looped her slender arms around his waist, and in that split second, the world skidded to grinding halt.

Suddenly he couldn't breathe. His mind was foggy with memories. He was eighteen again. The future was limitless, dreams firmly intact.

So quickly everything changed, setting them both on separate life paths.

He tightened his hold on Amber, allowing her to cry. He was glad she finally was able to release emotions she'd held on to for so long. At the same time, the pounding in his heart told him to keep his guard up. He was definitely treading on dangerous soil.

As she sobbed, Amber buried her head in his neck. He held her close, and the way she melted against him felt so right.

Too right.

This wasn't good.

Patrick took a deep breath and gave her a hard squeeze before loosening his hold on her. "I know it's been a tough few days."

"Yes, it has been," she muttered, separating herself from him. Instantly he missed the feeling of her warmth.

Digging deep for composure, Patrick shoved his hands into his pockets, conflicting emotions eating at him. There was a crazy person after Amber, and his job was to take that creep down. The last thing he needed was the distraction of his emotions.

Amber wiped away the last of her tears, and a slight smile appeared on her face, though it was tinged with sadness. Her stoic demeanor slipped back into place. "Thank you, Patrick, for everything you're doing to get this crime solved. It means a lot." She was looking up at him with those wide, beautiful eyes—twin pools of captivating warmth.

"You're welcome." Patrick nodded, searching for that

professional facade he needed to keep himself focused. All the while he was kicking himself for caving to an emotional moment.

He shouldn't have taken her in his arms.

And he wouldn't let it happen again.

SIX

Cavalier High School was located just outside the Savannah city limits. Patrick knew the route well, having gone there for four years. He took a side street off the highway, and then traveled several more miles before the school came into view. Amazingly, after all these years, it hadn't changed a bit. Even the designated areas for parking. He steered past the student lot and parked his SUV in a space marked for visitors.

As he approached the entrance, he felt an uneasy twinge. It had been eleven years since he'd left Cavalier as a high school track-and-field star with hopes of a bright athletic future. At that time, his classmates had pegged him to have a string of endorsement deals by the time he was twenty-two. They'd also voted him and Amber as the most likely couple to get married and add a half dozen little athletes to the world population.

He almost laughed at the silly polls. A lot had happened since then, and his classmates couldn't have been more wrong. Although at the time he half believed it.

In the school office, Patrick showed the receptionist his detective badge and asked to see Carl.

"Mr. Shaw is in class." The lady, whose name tag read Margie Hopper, frowned. "If you need to see him now, I'll have to send someone down to the gym to supervise his students while he talks to you."

Patrick wasn't dissuaded. "Okay."

With a sigh, Ms. Hopper pushed herself up from her chair and made her way to the back office. A step from the door she stopped, glanced back. "I hope this isn't about another speeding ticket he didn't pay."

Patrick gave a slight shrug. "I can't say, ma'am." Though Carl should be so fortunate.

He took a seat by the window to wait. The area was sparsely furnished. To his left sat a round table littered with college pamphlets. To his right, a few vinyl chairs were pushed up against the wall. This, too, looked like he remembered. Funny how some things never changed.

In contrast, his life was in a perpetual state of change. He never knew what God had in mind next.

Ten minutes into his wait Carl wandered into the office. He wore his blond hair military short, and a Cavalier High T-shirt clung to his muscular torso. "Margie, someone wanted to speak to me?"

Ms. Hopper said nothing, only jutted a finger in Patrick's direction.

"Good morning, Carl." Patrick stood.

Carl registered a look of surprise when he first turned, and then his face eased into a more pleasant expression. "Patrick Wiley. What on earth are you doing here?" He crossed the tile floor in two steps and extended his hand. "I had heard you joined the military."

Patrick shook Carl's hand. "You heard right. I served my time and now I work for the Savannah-Chatham Police Department."

"Good for you." Carl planted his legs apart, hands on his hips. "So to what do I owe the pleasure?"

"Is there some place private that we can talk?"

Carl narrowed his eyes warily. "Yeah. Sure. Everyone should be in class. We can talk outside if that's okay."

Patrick nodded.

As they walked out of the building, Carl glanced over

both shoulders and in front of him. "You know how rumors fly. I'm careful to keep my private business out of the gossip pool."

He obviously hadn't talked to Ms. Hopper. Patrick let that thought slide. "I understand."

Patrick followed Carl along the covered walkway, stopping when they got to the far side of the building.

Carl leaned up against a redbrick pillar, crossing his arms. "Okay, I know why you're here. But—" he flicked another nervous gaze around the area before meeting Patrick's head-on "—I can assure you that my attorney told me all charges had been dropped. I mean, if I missed the court date or something, I'm completely unaware."

Now Patrick was curious. The quick background check Liza had run on Carl revealed nothing significant. "What charges are you referring to, Carl?"

Carl leaned in. "The DWI." His voice dropped another octave. "I've had a few speeding tickets, but I swear to you, that DWI charge was bogus—"

"Woo, Carl." Patrick held up a staying hand. "This isn't about a DWI."

Carl drew back in surprise. "It's not?"

Patrick shook his head. "No. I'm here to talk to you about a particular party that your fraternity hosted."

"A college party?"

Patrick nodded. "One that took place your freshman year of college. It was an end-of-the-year bash."

"Freshman year?" Carl echoed, his voice slightly rising. "That's been forever ago. Why are you asking questions now?"

Patrick shifted his weight, half agreeing with Carl. The questions he needed to ask should have been addressed years ago, as well as bringing the culprit to justice. His stomach roiled at the thought. It was something he hoped to rectify soon. Patrick crossed his arms, kept his voice even. "We have reason to believe something that happened that night may be tied to the recent car-bombing case."

"Car bombing?" Carl straightened and pulled away from the pillar. "The one that involved Amber Talbot?"

"That's correct." While Patrick spoke, he studied Carl, searching his face, watching his body language. "I see you've been following the story."

Carl widened his stance, drew up his shoulders. "Yeah. I mean, it's been big news around here. Everyone's talking about it. I also read that Amber was attacked at her home by some unknown assailant." His brows scrunched together. "I feel bad for her, but I don't understand how any of that involves me."

That was what Patrick wanted to know, too. He shifted, cleared his throat. "Did you recall attending your fraternity's end-of-the-year party?"

Carl lowered his eyes and then looked straight at Patrick. "Yeah, I was there. Along with about half the freshman class."

Patrick held Carl's gaze boldly. "Tell me what you remember about that night in terms of Amber."

In a nonchalant move, Carl rested against the pillar again, hooking his thumbs into his belt loops. "Well, I guess, like the rest of us, Amber drank a little too much. She was stumbling around, not making any sense. A few of us guys started razzing her, you know, asking what you'd think about her out partying. That kind of stuff."

Patrick's hackles rose at the mention of Amber stumbling around. How many others that night assumed she'd had too much to drink? No one helped her, but someone definitely tried to take advantage of her. "So tell me, Carl, when you finished *razzing* Amber, what happened to her? Did she pass out? Leave the party? What?"

Shaking his head, Carl shrugged. "I don't know. Like I said, there were a lot of people there. I don't even recall seeing her after that."

"Did you ever hear anything about her afterward?"

Carl took a moment and then shrugged again, his bushy eyebrows low. "No, not that I can think of. Well, actually," he quickly amended, "I did hear that you guys broke up. Not that I was surprised, with her out partying like she was without you." He jutted a thick finger at Patrick. "You guys back together?"

Suddenly cold all over, Patrick felt the fine hairs on his neck spike. He was equally surprised and annoyed by the question and even more so by his reaction to it. He took a deep breath, putting his erratic emotions on hold. Something he'd have to deal with later.

"No, Amber and I are not back together." His tone had more bite than he intended. "However, I am the investigator on her case."

With a chuckle, Carl spread his hands, palms out. "Hey, I get it. Too personal."

He felt as if a fist had gripped his chest at Carl's flippant attitude. Then he saw it for what it was—a cheap attempt at diverting the conversation. That was not happening. "So, Carl, besides you, who else was harassing Amber at the party that night?"

"Harassing? Patrick." Carl's laugh was dry. "We never harassed her. We were just having a little fun."

At Amber's expense. Patrick's annoyance intensified. The muscles in his arms bunched. "Who are you referring to when you say *we*?"

Carl gave an offhand shrug. "Bruce Austin and Randall Becker. That's about it."

As expected. "Do you recall if either of them was ever alone with Amber? Or maybe offered to take her home?"

He shook his head. "We all stayed together. We actually ended up going to another party down the street later that night."

Patrick wasn't buying it. "So what's up with Randall these days? Do you see much of him?"

Carl hesitated for a split second then shook his head again. "Actually, I haven't seen much of Randall since college. After Bruce passed, well, we sort of lost touch." Carl spoke calmly, but his eyes and face couldn't hide his discomfort. "What's going on with Amber anyway?"

There he went again, diverting the conversation. Patrick folded his arms over his chest. "Someone attacked Amber the night of the frat party, and we have reason to believe that person may be after her now."

Carl jerked away from the pillar, his body rigid. "And you think I might be involved?"

Patrick didn't answer that. Instead, he put on a crooked smile and met Carl's eyes. "I'm just trying to get the facts together, Carl."

Relaxing his stance some, Carl nodded and carefully averted his gaze. "Good. Because I'm not privy to anything that happened to Amber Talbot eleven years ago or anything that's going on now. But I'm glad you're on the case. I have no doubt you'll catch whoever's been harassing her."

Harass. An interesting choice of words. Patrick gave Carl a firm pat on the shoulder before he turned to leave. "Rest assured, Carl, we're keeping an eye on everyone who had any contact with Amber that night. Including you."

Amber stapled the last Silence No More fund-raiser packet of information together. Settling back in her office chair, she flipped through one, skimming the list of vendors and pricing details while waiting for her colleagues Tony and Pam to arrive. She'd spent weeks compiling the data and it felt good to finally be finished.

By the time Tony walked into her office she had read through everything and was jotting a note, reminding herself to schedule a meeting with Penny, the community center's event planner, to firm up the agenda for the evening. Things were finally coming together—at least on paper.

Holding a half bagel in one hand and a cup of coffee in

the other, Tony settled into an armchair across from her, crossed one leg over his knee. "Afternoon, Amber." Before she could return the greeting, he lifted a brow. "It is a good afternoon, isn't it?"

"So far." Amber smiled. "No bombs or lurking bad guys. And plans for the fund-raiser are falling into place."

"That's great," Tony said around a mouthful of bagel. He washed it down with a swig of coffee. "You seem as if you're doing better, too. Good attitude in spite of the chaos going on in your life."

"I'm trying."

He lifted his cup in a toast. "Good for you. But if you need to talk, you know I'm here for you."

She nodded. It was a blessing to have Tony on staff at Safe Harbor. He was a true asset.

"Hope I'm not late." Pam Ralston poked her head into the office, a little out of breath. She worked part-time and was notoriously late. With two small kids and a pastor husband, she always had more to do than she had time for. Still Amber was happy to have her on staff.

"We're just getting started. Come on." Amber waved her in.

Pam took the chair beside Tony.

Amber handed them each a stapled packet. "This is an updated list of vendors, caterers, advertisers and such for the fund-raiser. I've also added names and contact information for the speakers and volunteers."

"Looks as though you have everything covered," Pam said, flipping through the packet.

Amber leaned in, folding her hands on the desk. "The itinerary for the evening is on the last page."

"Nice lineup." Tony nodded.

"Wait a minute." Pam caught Amber's gaze. "Your name isn't listed. Keynote speaker, right?"

"I'm still undecided on the right time to speak. Before dinner? After?" Amber tried to answer casually, although knowing someone from her past didn't want her to speak at all dampened her enthusiasm.

"Are you still considering sharing your story?" Tony always zeroed in on the heart of her issues. As if he could read her mind.

Amber gave a quick shrug.

Originally she'd planned a simple, informative talk. One that focused on recovery and preventative safety and shared her team's treatment styles and community resources. She'd tossed around the idea of sharing her own story. But what would be the point? Every victim in the audience understood abuse.

But now with her darkest memories exposed, maybe she should reconsider.

Anxiety twisted her stomach like a pretzel.

Then again, maybe not. She remembered how difficult it had been to open up to Tony a few weeks ago. Talking about that part of her life still wasn't easy.

"Why don't you speak while the bids are being tallied for the silent auction?" Pam suggested.

"That would be perfect, right before dessert." Tony grinned. "You'll still have a full house. Nobody leaves before cheesecake."

Amber laughed and grinned back at him. "Sounds good. At least I'll know you'll still be there." As she penciled it in on her itinerary, Pam added, "Hopefully by the fundraiser, your elusive stalker worries will be over."

Pam's comment brought Amber back to reality. The fund-raiser was in less than two weeks. What if her worries weren't over by then?

"Yes, let's hope so, Pam." Amber kept writing, her eyes trained on her paper as she scribbled more notes than were necessary, trying to regroup, think positively.

She couldn't remember ever working so hard or so long. Ten months of planning had gone into this fund-raiser. It had taken her weeks just to find someplace to hold it after talking to umpteen venues trying to secure the best prices. And she couldn't forget advertising. Brochures and pamphlets, stopping by businesses, making phone calls. Gritting her teeth, she scribbled harder.

The last thing she wanted was to postpone the fundraiser.

"You okay, Amber?" Tony's calm voice snapped her back.

She looked up and caught both Tony and Pam staring at her. "Sorry. Just a little reality-check moment. I still can't believe what's happening to me. If the bomb and being attacked in my own home weren't enough, now I have the fund-raiser on the line."

"Amber, if you have to postpone, it's not the end of the world." Pam sat at the edge of her seat. "You can always reschedule for fall."

"Fall?" She gritted her teeth, glancing between Pam and Tony. "I ordered pastel decor and blooming plants to use for centerpieces. Spring is a time for new beginnings."

"Whatever happens, kiddo," Tony assured her, "you'll make the best of it, you know that."

Yes, Amber sighed. She would get through this, unless of course, somebody killed her first. Rocking back in her seat, she pushed her fingers through her hair. She couldn't help but laugh at her sad predicament.

"Amber, I'm worried about you." Tony's low, measured voice usually soothed her, but not now. Disappointment and fear nibbled at her.

Amber rocked forward and shook her head. "Don't be worried about me. I'm going to be okay. A little frazzled, but okay. But until further notice, I prefer not to think about or discuss postponing the fund-raiser."

Her colleagues exchanged a look, but both agreed without protest. Amber breathed a little easier. She wasn't giving up yet. Two weeks gave Patrick plenty of time to hunt down the perpetrator.

She hoped.

* * *

When Patrick arrived at Coastal Karate School, he saw Randall Becker approaching the building from the opposite end of the parking lot. Tall and lean with chin-length dark curls, he looked about the same as he did in high school, outside of a few extra pounds of rock-solid muscle.

Leaning against his vehicle, Patrick crossed his arms and waited, finding it ironic that a kid who'd lost more fights than he'd won in high school was now a martial arts expert.

Randall passed Patrick with barely a glance. He stepped onto the sidewalk leading to the school.

Patrick pushed away from his SUV and started toward him. "Good afternoon, Randall."

A second's hesitation, then Randall pivoted around, his face like stone. "Patrick Wiley?" He shook his head. "So that was you. I'd hoped I was seeing things."

Patrick held his stare. "Sorry to disappoint you."

"Yeah, right." Randall scowled back at him, shoving his hands on his hips. "What can I do for you, Wiley?"

Unlike Carl Shaw, Randall Becker wasn't the type to waste time or words on being cordial. Rather, he jumped to the point. A behavior Patrick actually preferred over superficial geniality.

"Actually, I have a couple questions for you." Patrick started to flash his badge.

"I get it." Randall held up a hand and snickered. "Who would have guessed? The rising track star is now part of the cop squad."

"Gotta make a living." Patrick forced a small smile. "Can we talk someplace private?"

Randall's left eyebrow raised. "About?"

"Attempted murder."

His eyes turned cold. "What are you getting at, Wiley?"

Patrick glared back, unblinking. "The questions I have

for you aren't really appropriate to discuss in the parking lot of your school."

Randall huffed with disgust, turned and stalked toward the building, then jerked open the door. "Let's go."

Patrick accompanied him past several windowed studios where children of various ages dressed in martial arts garb eagerly practiced kicks and sparred while parents looked on. Across the hall, adults showed off more complex and powerful karate moves.

"Looks like a thriving business," Patrick said, following Randall down a short hall.

"It's been a lot of hard work." Randall stopped and unlocked a door. "So whatever you're here for, let's make it quick. I've got a class to teach."

Patrick followed Randall inside. The interior of the office reeked of musty sneakers and cheap cologne. Boxes of karate uniforms and fighting gear crowded the perimeter of the limited floor space. And a card table, serving as a makeshift desk, sat in the middle of the clutter, along with two white plastic chairs.

Randall gestured impatiently. "Have a seat and let's get this over with."

Patrick settled into one chair and Randall plopped onto the other, straddling it. Plunking his elbows on the seat back, he glared at Patrick, his dark eyes sparking with annoyance. "Okay. What do you want?"

"I'm here to discuss a particular college frat party."

"Frat party?"

"Yes. One that your fraternity put on. It took place the end of your freshman year."

A shrug, then a smirk. "We hosted parties all the time."

"I'm talking about an end-of-the-year bash. Freshman year," Patrick reiterated. "It was a pretty big deal. A lot of people attended."

Patrick sat back and waited for Randall to answer. He could imagine the wheels turning in that thick skull of his.

Trying to fend off suspicion by not reacting too quickly. Patrick knew his type well.

Suddenly, Randall's mouth twitched into a humorous grin. "Amber Talbot. Party-girl extraordinaire. Is that what this is about?"

Anger fisted tight in Patrick's gut at Randall's smug expression. It took all his control not to launch out of the chair and wipe that smirk off Randall's face. "Tell me what happened to Amber that night."

Randall lifted a shoulder in an offhanded shrug. "What's to tell? She showed up. Mingled around and drank too much."

Patrick's mouth tightened at his assumption. "You saw her drinking?"

Randall lifted a brow, paused. "I wasn't paying that close attention, but I saw the results. She was stumbling around, not making any sense."

Disgust twisted tighter in Patrick's stomach. "You may have assumed too much."

Randall's eyebrows snapped together. "What do you mean by that?"

"Somebody may have drugged Amber that night."

"Drugged?" Randall's smugness eased up some, but his mouth stayed in a straight, rigid line. "I don't know anything about that."

"Never heard any rumors? We both know guys talk."

Randall tipped the chair forward on two legs. "I heard nothing then, and I don't know what's going on with Amber now. I read the news. She obviously got on someone's bad side."

"Or maybe someone is afraid history will be revealed."

"What kind of history?" Randall's mouth puckered.

"Incriminating history."

"What do you think you have on me, Wiley?"

Patrick waited a beat, gave a thin smile. "Like I said,

Randall, I'm just asking questions. I'm not pointing fingers."

Randall came up out of his seat, the chair slamming to the ground. "Listen here, Wiley." He jabbed a finger in the air. "Whatever happened or is happening with Amber Talbot doesn't involve me."

Patrick stood, also. "One more question, then. Are you still friends with Carl Shaw?"

A short pause, then Randall shook his head. "No. Why?"

"Just trying to piece things together."

Randall gave Patrick a hard look, his teeth gritted. "Wiley, don't play games with me. Now that you've got a little power, you better not be trying to get back at me for something—"

"This isn't personal, Randall." Patrick held up a hand. "I'm just doing my job."

Randall screwed up his face. "Job or not, I want you to know I've got my act together now. I'm a black belt master and I own my own business. I can't afford for my name to get tied to anything criminal."

Patrick nodded. "Let's hope it won't have to be."

SEVEN

At five o'clock, Amber checked her emails one last time before powering down the computer as if it was just another day at work.

From the time she'd arrived that morning she'd been caught up in a flurry of activity. Her meeting with Tony and Pam and catching up with paperwork had prevented her from dwelling on the other major issues in her life. Like who was trying to kill her. And the way her heart pounded when Patrick Wiley was around.

She'd never met another man that affected her that way, or maybe she'd been too busy wrestling with the past to notice. An unsettling thought.

But even more disturbing, she'd never been bothered by the lack of romantic interests in her life. Until seeing Patrick again. He had seemed to move on just fine. Made a new life for himself. Something she had expected and regretted at the same time.

Sooner or later, she hoped to do the same.

Her phone rang and she picked it up. "Safe Harbor Counseling Center."

No answer.

"Hello?"

Click.

Chills trickled up her spine and she shivered. That was

the third hang-up today. She hung up the receiver. Everything had her antsy these days. Even a likely wrong number. She hated feeling as though she had to watch over her shoulder.

Even worse, she hated thinking that someone was watching her. Waiting for an opportunity to—

Enough. She tamped that thought down. It was hardly productive.

While she breathed out a sigh, she picked up her bag and left her office. She walked into the lobby and Patrick was there, seated in a wing chair waiting for her.

Nope. Nothing normal about this day.

With a glance at Amber, Patrick set down the magazine he was reading and stood. "Well, hello there."

"Hi, Patrick." Amber forced a nonchalant tone in her voice. "I thought we were meeting at the Riverside Café?"

"I finished work a little early. I stopped by to see if you were still here, and Tony let me in on his way out." Patrick moved around a potted plant and then closed the gap between them in two long strides.

Amber nodded, her emotions skittering between gratitude and bewilderment. It was a testament to Patrick's good character that his determination to catch her pursuer and keep her safe took precedence over even his free time.

Hopefully, his girlfriend didn't mind.

Another shiver came, skidding up her spine. She tamped it down and swallowed hard. "If you'd like, we can hang out here for a while and discuss the case. You probably want to get home and get some sleep after staying up all night in your car."

"Most of the night." He grinned. "I caught a few winks. Besides, nothing a cup of coffee won't fix. And with a lunatic on the loose, I expect a few more nights of surveillance will be in my future."

Amber winced at Patrick's mention of spending more

nights sitting in his SUV in front of Kim's house, watching over her. It was his job to investigate, she got that, but making sure she was safe around the clock? Surely that wasn't part of his job description. Then again, she remembered seeing on the news that the local police had been hit with a severe staffing shortage. Too few officers to do the job, and everyone worked overtime to fill the gaps.

That explained it.

Patrick's attentiveness wasn't personal. It was his job. Too bad he didn't realize what *doing his job* did to her haywire emotions.

She flipped back her hair, chagrin registering as she thought about that morning. Her guard had not only slipped, but also completely unraveled the moment Patrick had wrapped his strong arms around her.

Wholeheartedly, she'd fallen into his embrace, reveling in the warmth of his touch and the protective feeling it brought. Albeit, her legs had been wobbly, literally quaking at the knees, but she still should have stepped away, kept her composure intact.

"Okay, let's go get that coffee, then." She grabbed her keys from her purse. Obviously she was the sleep-deprived one.

Amber shut off the lights and headed for the door.

As Patrick started to follow, three sharp pops lit the air, one after another. Glass shattered.

Gunfire!

Amber jerked back around with a shriek.

"Get down!" Patrick yelled, but he didn't wait. He barreled toward her, taking her to the ground himself.

Another series of bullets whizzed through the plate glass, blowing out half the front window.

For the first time in his life, sheer, cold terror infiltrated every vein and touched every nerve. His adrenaline shot to the red zone. Whoever this creep was, he wasn't going to get his hands on Amber. "You need to get into the hallway," he ordered. "Away from the glass."

The color drained from her face as her wide eyes locked on to his. "Okay."

Another round of shots blasted into the building.

Patrick stayed beside her as they belly crawled deeper into the building, shielding her from the threat of more gunfire.

Once there, he shoved his cell phone into her hand. "Call 9-1-1 and stay down. Tell them I need backup now, but no lights or sirens."

She nodded before she started punching the numbers.

Cautiously raising himself up, Patrick slipped his hand into his jacket pocket, molded his fingers around his revolver.

A fourth array of shots sent more splintered glass raining into the room.

Staying low, Patrick edged to the door. Wedging himself between the doorjamb and wall, he kicked the door open and whipped out his weapon. This guy was his. He squinted, his vision searching the street and buildings beyond.

Muffled sirens sounded, blaring closer. Too close. A second later, scores of squad cars roared from both directions, tires screeching against asphalt as they slammed to a stop in front of the counseling center.

No way! Patrick gritted his teeth and beat a fist against the doorjamb, knowing the guy had hightailed it out of there.

At the police department, Patrick ushered Amber through the violent crimes investigation department under the speculative glances of the desk sergeant and other detectives, stopping when they arrived at the detective squad room.

"I need to check on a couple things. You can have a seat in my office." Patrick gestured toward a door marked Lead Detective Patrick Wiley. Any other day Patrick's title would have impressed Amber, and she would have said so, but between the wave of nausea churning in her midsection and the mind-boggling numbness dulling her brain, her ability to stand, much less think, was sorely in jeopardy.

"Thank you, I'll wait in there." She nodded, and then managed on shaky legs to walk in that direction while Patrick stepped aside to have a conversation with another officer.

Once inside, Amber slipped off her jacket and sank into one of the worn vinyl armchairs opposite his desk and tried to ignore the chaos rumbling just outside the room. The chatter of detectives, phones ringing and keyboards clacking made for a cacophony of activity.

Even after six in the evening, the staff stayed busy working to keep Savannah safe. Once this ordeal was over she'd have to write the department a nice letter telling them how much she appreciated their service.

That was if *over* meant she'd still be around.

A shiver snaked up her spine. Whoever was after her was persistent and cunning, which made her wonder what he had planned next.

She rubbed at the goose bumps on her arms and took in a deep, cleansing breath. Patrick was on it, looking at clues, trying to fit the pieces together even as she sat there.

She only hoped that would be enough.

Pushing that last thought aside, she tried to find the words to pray. If ever she needed God's help, it was now. She squeezed her eyes shut and waited. No words came. Just the same oppressive sadness that never strayed far, holding her hostage since her world had imploded eleven years ago.

She slumped down in her seat and shook her head. The

feeling hammered home just how much her one mistake had cost her—a future with Patrick and her faith.

Tears clogged her throat and she sniffed, knowing in about twenty seconds she was about to break down and cry. The last thing she wanted to do was wallow in that little black hole of regret her life had become.

No. She toughened up, seizing on that regret and using it to fuel her determination to keep it together. She would not let that creep get to her.

She was safe. For now that was enough.

Somewhat better, Amber made a conscious effort to relax. Shifting against the cushions, she glanced around the room, taking in every detail. It was a rather small space, made smaller by the overflowing clutter. Besides Patrick's oversize desk, dozens of boxes of evidence had been stacked to the ceiling, competing for floor space with mounds of law enforcement journals and boxed files marked Confidential. Two file cabinets, topped with folders and more paperwork, sat below the tall single window that provided a splash of sunlight through half-open blinds.

The room definitely had a chaotic element, and it was about half the size and twice the clutter as in the movies. But this was the real deal. A detective's office. Her detective.

She bit back a sigh.

After a few more moments, Patrick stepped into the room and closed the door. "Would you like some coffee? Or something to eat?"

Adrenaline kept her heartbeat thumping. The last thing she needed was caffeine. Then again, it would be a long night. "Nothing to eat, but coffee would be nice."

Patrick circled his desk, plopped into the swivel chair and picked up the phone. He flicked a glance at her. "Cream, no sugar, right?"

"Yes, thank you." Amber told herself it was of no significance that he remembered how she liked her coffee. She remembered that he liked his black, which meant nothing, either.

Patrick settled back against the sturdy wood frame of his chair and folded his arms. "Let me bring you up to speed on what's going on. Right now, forensics is at the scene trying to identify the bullets used. We're also interviewing employees and patrons from the neighboring shops to see what they know."

She managed a nod.

"And we've contacted everyone on the list you gave me this morning and got a statement from them."

Amber detected a tiny note of hope in his tone. She sat up straighter. "Did they tell you anything that might help?"

His eyebrows went up. "To be honest, most folks didn't recall the party. And those who did had a vague memory at best. With the exception of your old roommate. She remembered you chatting with three guys at the party."

"So she substantiated my story?"

"Yes." He nodded. "However, she was pretty oblivious about anything else that went on with you that night."

"She left for home early the next morning, before I was released from the hospital. I never told her what happened." Amber's heart sank. "So I guess your effort was a bust?" A pretty uneventful evening for everyone but her.

Patrick gave an offhanded shrug. "Not necessarily. Her statement helps us, and as far as the others, sometimes people deny knowledge of something, then a guilty conscience entices them to call back."

"That would be nice."

"Yes, it would." Patrick nodded, and then added, "Regardless, we're pushing forward, centering our focus on Randall and Carl. I spoke to both of them today."

Stress caused a little twist in her stomach at just hearing their names. "And what did they have to say?"

"Exactly what I expected." He gave her a subtle grin. "They both denied knowledge of anything."

The door swung open and a uniformed woman appeared. She handed one cup of coffee to Patrick and one to her. "Here you go."

"Thank you." Amber wrapped her palms around the cup, savoring the warmth, as the woman stepped back out.

Patrick set his coffee aside, grabbed a laptop from his bag and powered it on. "I have something to show you." He positioned the computer for her to see. "Liza, our criminologist, gathered some data about our two suspects, Randall and Carl."

Liza. Amber blew out an uneasy breath. The blonde date from last night.

He typed in "Talbot File" and the tense knot in Amber's midsection coiled tighter as a dozen pictures popped up on the screen. Black-and-white shots ranging from the parking lot crime scene taken minutes after the bombing, to her home, sectioned off with caution tape, and various rooms inside.

She breathed a little easier when Patrick scrolled farther down the page and new photos came into view.

"These are Randall's and Carl's senior photos. See if anything about them jogs your memory. Their build, their features. Anything."

Amber's gaze skimmed each photo. Countless memories about that night were still vivid. Yet as many or more remained a blur in her mind. "Sorry. Nothing new jumps out at me."

"That's okay." Patrick nodded. "Take a good look at these." He clicked on the mouse, enlarging the photos of Carl and Randall. Another click and recent shots of the men emerged onto the screen. "Then and now. Maybe you've seen one of them lurking around."

Amber stared at the screen. For the past eleven years

she'd worked hard to block the memories. Rehashing them equaled pain, like slowly ripping a scab off a wound. Now here she was racking her brain, trying to give her attacker a name.

"Well?" Patrick scooted his chair closer to his desk, hopefulness in his expression.

"I don't know." Amber tilted her head and leaned in, studying each man more closely. Carl's short cropped hair, broad smiling face, hollow stare. No one ever knew what he was thinking. Friendly, agreeable, hostile or argumentative, his mood changed depending on the company he kept. Randall, on the other hand, feared nothing. He spoke his mind without reserve, picked fights and was suspended more times than anyone in high school. Amber took in the loose dark curls that grew over his collar, his crooked smile, dark beady eyes.

Her mind bounced from one thought to another as she forced herself to delve into her memory, searching for any snippet of information that would make either one of the men stand out.

She sat back, shrugged. "Sorry, Patrick. Nothing."

The hopefulness in his expression faded, leaving nothing but murkiness in its wake. "Amber, dig deep," Patrick persisted. "Think about that night. Wasn't there something that stood out? A voice? A laugh? Anything?"

Amber held Patrick's gaze across the desktop, feeling strangely at a loss. Patrick wasn't going to be happy until she gave him conclusive facts. Of which she had none. "Patrick—" she sighed "—so much of that night is still foggy. Honestly, I've told you everything I remember."

Patrick lifted a finger, for emphasis, no doubt, but dropped it when there was a knock on the door. He glanced over her shoulder. "Come on in."

Amber breathed relief. If he thought that by pointing out the urgency of the situation she could just will herself into remembering some kind of concrete evidence, he was dead wrong.

She completely understood the urgency, and the memories that scrambled her brain were bad enough.

The door creaked open. A man she recognized stuck his head in. Vance Peterson, another classmate from high school.

"Hey, Patrick, do you mind if I interrupt?" Vance said.

"Sure. Come on in, Captain." Patrick eased back in his chair, folded his arms. "Amber, you remember Vance? He supervises this department and is the culprit who enticed me to quit the navy and come back to Savannah. He's also the man I answer to."

"I see." Amber nodded. "How are you, Vance?"

"Doing fine." Vance stepped inside. He focused his gaze on Amber and placed his hands on his hips. "I hope you know how fortunate you are to have Patrick on your case. It took some hefty persuasion to get him here, but he's the best investigator on the force."

"Persuasion?" Patrick erupted with a hardy laugh. "Don't you mean pleading and groveling?"

"Okay. I'll give you *pleading*. But *groveling*? Come on." Vance sprouted the same impish grin.

The thick blond hair from his teens had now aged into a medium brown. He still wore it short, with soft spikes on top. Not quite as tall as Patrick, he stood about five-ten, with broad shoulders and a muscled physique.

Amber smiled. Patrick and Vance had been friends since junior high. They'd been an inseparable duo. They both were athletic, charming and funny. She'd always enjoyed the camaraderie between them. Seeing them together reminded her of better times.

"So tell me what's happening on the case." Vance's deep baritone took on a serious lilt as he morphed back into police-captain mode.

Patrick rocked forward in his chair. "You know about the shots fired at Amber's counseling center?"

Vance nodded. "I heard it got hit pretty hard."

"Oh, yeah, there's some damage, all right." Patrick grimaced and added, "Blew out the front window and fractured the facade of the building."

Amber pressed one hand to her churning stomach. Somehow hearing the details made the truth that much more chilling. This guy wasn't playing.

"But of course, those things are easily repaired," Patrick said, giving her an affable yet serious look. Probably his way of reassuring her. Keeping her from a major meltdown.

Smart man.

"Brick, mortar and glass are easy to fix." Vance crossed his arms. "Finding this guy seems to be our problem. But we need to get him off the street before he actually hurts someone. What do you have on the suspects?"

"We're making progress." Patrick opened a file to read from his notes. "Liza did a little searching and found some pertinent data. Carl and Randall both have more history than originally thought. Carl, in fact, was issued a restraining order in college for stalking a former girlfriend. The charges were eventually dropped."

"Dropped or not, that's pretty significant." Vance scratched his chin. "What about Randall?"

"Last month, his wife filed divorce papers. Adultery and domestic abuse were cited as grounds."

"Nice guy." Vance paused, his deep-set eyes narrowing as he stared at the computer screen. "So what is your gut telling you?"

"My instincts say one or both are involved." Patrick shook his head. "Which one or to what degree, I've yet to determine."

"What about you?" Vance's gaze cut from the screen to Amber.

She gave a tiny shrug. "I don't have a gut feeling about much these days. This included."

Vance nodded. "I'm sure this whole ordeal is quite disturbing. I'm sorry you're in the middle of this."

"Thank you, Vance." Amber mustered up a tight smile.

"What about you, Captain?" Patrick asked. "What's your take?"

Vance exchanged a look with Patrick. "No call on this one yet. Carl and Randall both grew up on the edge of trouble, but assault and attempted murder?" Vance glanced at Amber, brow knit. "I attended a couple of those frat parties myself. Things got crazy sometimes, but for either of those guys to be so cruel to a woman is—"

"Totally possible," Patrick interrupted.

After a short pause, Vance gave a shrug, and nausea swirled in Amber's stomach. "You're exactly right."

"Unfortunately, capable doesn't equal guilty." Patrick emitted a deep sigh. "But both of them know they're being watched. And the moment one slips up…I've got them."

EIGHT

Later that night, Amber's eyes drifted to the faint glow of the alarm clock. Two hours she'd been in bed, every moment plagued with mounting frustration. After tossing and turning and staring at the ceiling, she was now more awake than ever. She'd tried counting sheep, reading, pacing and even taking a hot shower, trying to relax.

Still she couldn't sleep. Her mind was too busy spinning scenarios. Conjuring up a litany of what-ifs and maybes. Who was her attacker…and what if she accused the wrong man? Maybe the gut feeling she'd had about Randall, Bruce and Carl was wrong?

Sighing, she rubbed her face. She was getting nowhere. Blunting the memories was far easier than trying to remember.

But Patrick wanted answers. Something definitive.

There had to be something. A word, a scent, some memory.

Crimping her eyes, she forced herself to think, focus, push her thoughts back to that dingy frat room.

She drew in a deep breath, then exhaled slowly as she let her mind drift back. Eleven years, to that unforgettable night…

A small room. Dark. The whir of a ceiling fan. The air oppressive, stale. With effort, she'd managed to grip her fingers along a table edge or desk. She was confused, dazed, wondering how she got there. Music played in the background. Classical. Eerie. Pain boomeranged in her skull. Claustrophobia swallowed her, the walls closing in.

Then she heard him. His voice was high and singsong—a phony disguised lilt. She tried to place it. Tried to replay his words in her head. *Patrick.* He kept talking about Patrick. Where was he now? Who was going to save her?

Then the man laughed. The most chilling laugh she'd ever heard.

Panic grew. Blood turned to ice. She forced her trembling legs to run. Her hands frantically slapped walls, furniture to guide her to escape…

Until strong arms grabbed her, keeping her from going anywhere.

Amber's eyes blinked open, her heart galloping in her chest, a sheen of cold sweat filming her skin. She couldn't do this tonight. Nighttime was always the worst.

Now more antsy than ever, she got out of bed. Lying still a moment longer was definitely out of the question. In an attempt to stave off the shiver that began in her very soul, she grabbed her robe and paced the room, each firm step adding to her stress.

She just wanted to wake up one day and have this nightmare be over.

Chilly air from the air conditioner wafted around her, pulling her back to the present. She stopped short as rational thoughts took hold.

She'd never stopped to consider how much worse things could have been. Maybe God had intervened before the situation had escalated further.

She was nearly blown away by the concept. The tension knotting her muscles started to ease, replaced by a strange peaceful feeling.

Slipping back into bed, she snuggled beneath the blankets. There was a gentle snore from down the hallway. She curled up tighter, glad Patrick could finally sleep. When Kim had suggested he bunk on her living room sofa for the night instead of his SUV, he'd jumped at her offer.

His dedication astounded her. She didn't deserve that.

It seemed ironic that Patrick was determined to protect her from the very madman who had pushed their life into a tailspin eleven years ago.

Or could it be that in spite of her severed relations with God, He had sent this elite soldier and detective back into her life?

Even if it was a temporary assignment for Patrick, her heart melted at the thought.

Hit by the first rays of morning light streaming through the slats of the window blind, Patrick squinted and checked his watch. Barely past six. He pulled the sheet over his head, tempted to roll over and keep on sleeping. Had he not heard somebody up and rumbling around in the kitchen, he might have done so.

Sitting up, Patrick swung his feet to the floor, every muscle in his back as tight as rubber bands. Apparently, his body's way of protesting for two nights of awkward sleeping arrangements.

But despite being stiff, he'd slept okay, although lightly, with one ear attuned to his surroundings.

The night had been peaceful. No bells or whistles from the security system. Nothing unusual to note. Outside of the periodic pattering of soft footsteps coming from Amber's room down the hall. She was restless and he didn't blame her—she was dealing with a lot.

Hopefully his presence offered her some solace and a sense of safety.

With a low groan, he rubbed at the cramp in his side. Over the years he'd slept in more confined and uncomfortable quarters. He almost felt like a wimp missing his own bed with the nice memory-foam mattress. *Guess that's what civilian life does to someone.*

Patrick rose slowly, stretching his arms over his head and yawning. *Better.* He cracked his knuckles.

Now he was ready to start the day. A slight clanking came from across the hall, accompanied by a whiff of something savory.

Breakfast.

A low growl in his gut responded. He hefted the knapsack he'd brought in from his car and headed to the bathroom to change his clothes and clean up. Then he went to check out what was cooking.

In the kitchen doorway, he paused and, as Amber moved around the small space, he did a quick survey of the area. The round mahogany table sat empty, pantry open, nothing lurking in the corners.

Turning slightly, he glanced out the wide bay window by the table, his gaze traveling beyond the front yard to the neighborhood street. A minivan puttered along going east, and right behind it a patrol vehicle.

Good. They were making rounds, just like he requested. He loved those guys.

Satisfied, he settled his gaze back on Amber. Humming softly, she continued cooking, her damp hair tumbling over her shoulders. Her pastel sundress clung softly to her curves, her feet bare.

The sight unleashed more unbidden feelings. Ones he'd kept locked up for years.

Patrick's mouth edged up as he watched her, hesitant to interrupt, reveling in the peaceful moment. He couldn't help but admire her beauty.

No other woman had ever affected him the way Amber Talbot did. Too much time with this woman and he'd be a goner.

A lump crowded into his throat. At one time he'd hoped for a scenario like this. Sharing a quiet morning with Amber—sharing a lifetime together.

He remembered how she loved to cook. And how she used to surprise him with new recipes when they'd dated. He'd tease her about opening a restaurant. She'd respond that she only enjoyed cooking for him.

That was forever ago. His heart thumped in his chest.

Amber turned and grabbed an egg from a carton on the counter. With a gasp, she jumped, her eyes going wide, the egg dropping to the floor. "Patrick. You scared me to death." Her splayed fingers slapped her chest.

So much for not being obvious. "Sorry. I didn't mean to sneak up on you." Patrick grabbed a handful of napkins from the table. "Let me clean that up."

"No. I've got it." Amber tore a paper towel from a roll, squatted down and sopped up the gooey mess.

"I should have said something. I wasn't thinking." He'd been too busy reminiscing. Something he shouldn't be doing.

"I'm just a little jumpy these days." She tossed the soiled towels into the trash and turned on the faucet to wash her hands.

"As you should be. By the way, whatever you're cooking smells great."

"It's just bacon, eggs and toast," Amber said, turning from the sink. She leaned against the cabinet and wiped her hands on a dish towel. "I thought you might be hungry."

She'd thought right. He smiled. "It sounds delicious. What can I do to help?"

"Nothing. Just have a seat and relax."

Once he was up and about, *relax* wasn't in his vocabulary these days.

"On second thought, you can grab some plates." With her chin, she gestured to the cabinet to her left.

"Two? Three? What do we need?"

"Only two. Kim won't be joining us. It's her day off and she's sleeping in."

Not that it mattered if they ate alone, although he didn't mind. He gathered the plates, and as Amber finished scrambling the eggs, he grabbed two cups of freshly brewed coffee and took them to the table.

"Here you go." Amber set one plate in front of him and another on the place mat across the table before she settled into her seat.

"Do you mind if I say a blessing?" he asked her.

After a slight hesitation she shrugged. "Sure."

They bowed their heads.

"Lord, please let this food bless and nourish our bodies. And thank You for our many blessings. Amen."

"Amen," she mumbled.

"And keep Amber safe." Patrick met Amber's gaze, smiled.

"Thank you." Amber gave him one of those squinty-eyed smiles. The one that meant she was trying to not cry.

He took a bite of his food. Amber's safety was on the top of his prayer list these days. He hoped his simple prayer might touch her some. He'd noticed her faith didn't seem what it once had been.

"You know, you're a pretty brave woman," he said after a moment, lifting his coffee cup to his lips.

"Brave?" A slight laugh escaped her. "I hardly think *brave* is the best description of me."

"Oh, but you are. With all that is going on, you haven't let it get you down." He shoved a bite of eggs in his mouth and nodded.

She shook her head, staring sullenly into her cup of coffee, where she'd just stirred a serving of cream. "For over a decade I kept a painful secret from you. I gave in to fear and guilt. I feel anything but brave."

Her rationale hit him like a blow. Was he to blame for her fear? Maybe if he hadn't been such a hothead, maybe if she had trusted him more—

No. He refused to go there again. He took a sip of coffee, set the cup down carefully, so as not to give away the turmoil churning inside him. *Lord, give me the wisdom to break through the wall of guilt she's erected.*

"Amber, you became victim to a vicious, selfish act. It's understandable how fear and guilt could clog your mind after something like that. But look at you now. You've dedicated your life to helping others. I admire that."

Five seconds later, he regretted the words when Amber glanced up at him. Her expression of raw pain and remorse tore at his heart.

"Patrick, you can't minimize the mistakes I've made."

What he couldn't minimize was the guilt she was carrying.

Silence settled between them. He forked another bite of eggs, watching Amber out of the corner of his eye.

For the past several moments she had been toying with her nearly full plate of food. His attempt at being supportive had batted zero. She obviously didn't want his understanding, only his help.

Truth be known, he was still trying to make sense of it all. Relieve some of the pain that had whittled away at him for years. Little by little, piece by piece, until he went numb.

And here he was, thrown back into Amber's life, his battered emotions spewing out like molten lava. Weakening him. Making him crazy.

He kicked himself for letting his guard slip so easily. So quickly. Again.

Before he got more caught up in his frustration, the ringtone sounded on his phone. He plucked it from his belt clip, thankful for the distraction. "This is Patrick Wiley."

"Good morning, Patrick. I have some news." His ears perked at Liza's words.

"Something good, I hope."

"Good for you. However, bad for Carl Shaw."

"Carl? What about him?"

"Well, he was picked up and brought into the station last night. A call came in that a vehicle was swerving on Highway 80 east. When an officer attempted to pull Carl over, he took off, leading them on a fourteen-mile chase before he ran off the road and into a ditch."

His lips curved at Liza's words. "Where is Carl now?"

"Sitting in a holding cell, waiting for his bail hearing. Here's the added bonus—they found four loaded guns in his trunk. A shotgun, two semiautomatic assault rifles and a handgun. We checked the registration, and they all belong to Shaw. We're running a ballistics test to see if any of the weapons match the bullets fired at the Safe Harbor Counseling Center."

"Excellent. I'll be right over. Thanks, Liza."

He ended the call and met Amber's wide stare with a grin. "We need to get going. I think we may have just hit pay dirt."

NINE

Amber paced from the narrow window in Patrick's office to his oak desk and then back again. She mentally counted her steps, trying for distraction, to kill time. Anything to keep from looking at her watch again.

From her last glance, only forty-five minutes had elapsed since Patrick left for the interrogation room. It seemed like hours.

Her attempt to sit calmly and wait for him to return abated in about ten seconds, just long enough for her mind to whip up images of Carl Shaw. The man who may be trying to kill her.

The man who may have assaulted and drugged her…

No. She picked up her pace, refusing to relive that experience with Carl.

After years of anonymity, she wasn't sure if she was ready to learn the identity of her attacker.

Besides, what if it wasn't Carl?

On the fifteen-minute ride to the station, Patrick had stayed on the phone with the forensics lab. The four weapons found in Carl's truck were the newest pieces of information that could tie him to the crime.

The gleam in Patrick's eyes told her he was ready to break the case.

Was he confident or hopeful? She'd soon find out.

Muffled voices bled into the office from the other side of the closed door. One deep tone erupted from amid the cacophony and caught her attention.

She halted her repetitive march and turned as the door swung open. Captain Vance Peterson, carrying two cups, walked in, looking concerned. "Amber, how are you doing?"

"I'm okay." She attempted a reassuring smile. "Any news about Carl?"

"He's agreed to answer questions. Actually, he requested to talk to Patrick, but only with his attorney present. We're waiting on him to arrive now." He handed Amber a cup of coffee. "Patrick said you drank yours with only cream."

"Yes, thank you." She gently blew on the hot liquid. "So Patrick hasn't seen Carl yet?"

"Not yet. But it shouldn't be long."

She curled her hands around the cup, absorbing the warmth. "Guilty or innocent, I suppose everyone wants an attorney to be present."

"Actually we prefer to interrogate suspects before they ask for an attorney. But we'll take what we can get." Vance lifted a brow. "Sorry about the wait. I know it's tough. Especially under the circumstances."

"Circumstances?"

"Someone has been trying to kill you."

"Yes. Of course." She took a sip of coffee, willing her knees not to buckle.

"Why don't you sit down?" Vance suggested, pointing her to a chair. "You look a little pale."

"I'm okay." She spoke lightly and smiled, trying to downplay her anxiety. "I just want this culprit found. I'm getting a little tired of having a target on my back."

"I can understand that. In the meantime, try to relax. I could probably scrounge up a newspaper if you'd like to read something."

"No, but thanks." Seeing her name slathered across the headlines wasn't exactly relaxing.

"Okay." Vance drained his cup and tossed it in the trash can. "Just remember whether Carl Shaw is our man or not, Patrick is diligent. One way or another, he'll get this case solved."

"I'm sure he will."

The shrill ringtone on Vance's phone sounded. He held the cell to his ear, listened a second and then gave a brisk nod. "I'll be right there.

"Shaw's attorney is here," he said, turning to leave.

Amber's heart kicked up as Vance walked out and shut the door behind him. Her thoughts returned to Carl Shaw. If he turned out to be her attacker, the thought of someday facing him in a courtroom was daunting.

As her legs turned to rubber again, Amber leaned on the edge of Patrick's desk. She took a couple cleansing breaths, and even as dread knotted in her stomach, she stomped out any speculation. Innocent until proved guilty, she reminded herself. And as of now, Carl Shaw was innocent.

Shaw's attorney, an overweight, balding man in his late fifties, pushed back in his chair and crossed his arms firmly over his chest the moment Patrick walked in the room. His stare met Patrick's. "Remember, Carl," he told his client, "you're not on trial here. You have the right to remain silent."

So the attorney was here to intimidate. Patrick smiled inside. No problem.

A few feet from the table, Patrick paused and zeroed his gaze on Carl, who sat beside his bulldog lawyer. Shoulders slumped forward and a scowl on his face, Carl looked about ready to crack. "He's right, Carl, anything you say or do can be used against you in a court of law." Patrick threw in that Miranda reminder before the attorney did. He liked everything out in the open. "By the way," he said, addressing the attorney, "I'm Patrick Wiley, lead detective."

The portly man nodded. "Stu Gilbert, a longtime friend of the Shaw family. And please note that I strongly oppose my client's decision to talk to you." Then in the next breath, he added, "And I assure you Mr. Shaw has done nothing that would suggest a tie to the recent murder attempts on Amber Talbot."

"I appreciate your confidence, Mr. Gilbert. Although, Carl hasn't been charged, nor has a connection been officiated." *Yet.* Patrick shifted his weight. "Still, I'm glad Carl has agreed to talk to us."

"Which again, I don't recommend."

Straightening in his seat, Carl glanced at his attorney. "Stu, I wanted you here as a friend and witness to what is talked about, not to stop me from talking."

Stu didn't look happy. And Patrick doubted he just planned to listen.

Patrick took a seat directly across from Carl. He planted an elbow on the table, rested his chin on his fist. "Okay, Carl, if you're ready to talk, I need to make you aware that this conversation is being videotaped."

Carl struggled to swallow. In a gesture of nervousness, his Adam's apple rode the length of his throat. "I guess that's okay."

"Then let's start with the police chase."

Carl shrugged without meeting Patrick's eyes. "I saw the cop car behind me, but I wasn't speeding or anything, so I guess it didn't register that he was following me."

"You didn't see flashing lights?"

"Not initially."

Patrick pulled the police report from his pocket and tossed it on the table. "It states here that after you ran a red light, you pulled onto Highway 80 east, where a fourteen-mile chase ensued. You were clocked in excess of eighty miles an hour."

Silence stretched for about twenty seconds as Carl slouched farther in the chair. "By the time I realized what was going on, sirens were blaring. Red, blue and white lights filled my rearview window. I got scared."

"Scared of what, Carl?"

This drew a dark scowl from Attorney Stu. "You don't have to answer that, Carl."

Carl ignored him. "Maybe *scared* isn't the right word. I was just caught off guard."

"You ran from the police, because you were *caught off guard*?" Patrick leaned in, his palms on the table. "Carl, in about two hours you're going to an arraignment hearing. Unless you come up with a better excuse than that, you'll have plenty of time to think of one in the county lockup."

"I refuse to have my client subjected to threats." Stu went rigid in his seat, his annoyance obvious.

"Just stating the possibilities, Mr. Gilbert." Patrick kept his eyes on Carl as he addressed the attorney.

"Okay." Carl's voice went low. "I'd had a couple drinks. I didn't want another DWI."

Mistrusting his explanation as well as his placid expression, Patrick looked at him square in the eye. "Interesting concept, Carl, except that your breath-alcohol level came up under the legal limit."

"I know that now."

"Come on, Carl, there's something missing to this puzzle. No one takes a cop on a high-speed chase for a possible DWI. Maybe it has more to do with the loaded guns in your trunk?"

Carl raised his head, eyes rounded. He looked over at Stu and then back at Patrick. "The guns were a gift from an old girlfriend. They're registered to me. I use them for target practice."

"Target practice?" Patrick shook his head and leaned forward. "So you drive around town with loaded guns in your trunk to use for target practice?"

"I was at the shooting range over the weekend and I had forgotten about the extra baseball practice I'd scheduled for my team. Once I remembered, I left in a hurry."

"Seems like a rather careless maneuver, don't you think, tossing loaded guns in your trunk?"

"Yeah...probably." Carl shrugged again.

"Of course, so does running from the police."

"Carl." His attorney's voice was low, but firm. "You're not helping yourself here."

Carl looked back and forth from his attorney to Patrick. Beads of sweat dotted his forehead. "Doesn't anyone understand? If I get another DWI, I can lose my job."

Crossing his arms, Patrick studied Carl a minute, watching the overhead light play over his grimacing features. After four hours locked up in a holding cell and another waiting for his attorney to arrive, he looked haggard, with bags under his eyes. Sure, he was tired, but he had to be sobered up completely by now. Which should make him sharp enough to recall that he was being investigated in the recent murder attempts on Amber. Yet he was rambling about a possible DWI.

"Carl, do you understand why you're being questioned today?"

Carl sniffed and took a swipe at his nose. "You think I have something to do with the murder attempts on Amber Talbot."

"That's right, and running from police coupled with having loaded guns in your trunk doesn't look good for you. Do you understand what I'm saying?"

Before Stu could open his mouth to object to the comment, Carl jumped up and slammed his broad palm down on the table. "No, Wiley! Listen up and understand this—I'm not your man!"

Good. Patrick bit back a smile, glad to see a fracture in Carl's victim facade.

"Carl, calm down. I think you've said enough." Stu half rose from his seat and gestured with his hands for Carl to sit back down.

Breathing heavily, Carl hesitated for a second and then reclaimed his seat.

His jaw clenched with his next argument. "Wiley, do you really think that if I was trying to kill someone, I would keep the evidence in my trunk?"

Patrick calmly sat there, folded his hands on the table. "People have done crazier things, Carl."

"Well, not me."

"Then why would you run?"

After a minute of hard silence, Carl fell back against the chair. He rubbed his hands over his face. "Drugs. Okay?" he mumbled. "Marijuana. Black tar heroin. I threw the bag out the window when I turned onto the highway."

Drugs? The unexpected confession jerked away any hope of a speedy resolution to Amber's case. Patrick took a deep breath, restraining his disappointment. "Do you sell or use?"

Carl sat up, gave him a pointed look. "Do you know how hard it is to live on a teacher's salary?"

That answered it. And Patrick wasn't about to tread down that path. He'd leave that up to the narcotics task force. Now for a last-ditch effort for his case. "Have you been trying to kill Amber Talbot, Carl?"

"No!"

"Then who, Carl?"

"Carl, that's enough." There was some heat in his attorney's voice now.

Carl shifted in his chair. His gaze flicked to the older

man, then back to Patrick. "How could I guess that, Patrick?"

"No hunch?"

"None."

They were getting nowhere. "All right," Patrick conceded. "What about the frat house party?"

"I told you before. I don't know anything about that, either."

"Come on, Carl, spare me the litany of denials." Patrick raised his voice on that one. "Guys talk. You lived at the house. You had to have heard something."

Carl sat silent for several seconds, his thick brows pulling tight over his eyes. "Even if I did, who believes rumors anyway?"

Patrick scooted to the edge of his seat. "What kind of rumors, Carl?"

"Just rumors," Carl said with a shrug. "Big talk. Who knows what's true."

"Some people do believe rumors, don't they, Carl?"

His face went blank, wiped clean of all expression.

"Carl, don't say any more." Stu's warning went unnoticed and Patrick barreled forward.

"It's fair to assume that if Amber spoke publicly about what happened to her the night of the frat party, even without names, somebody might be able to fill in the blanks. And that would scare somebody with something to hide. Wouldn't it, Carl?"

Carl's cold eyes locked on Patrick for a second. "Whatever Amber chooses to speak about wouldn't involve me."

"Who would it involve, Carl…based on rumors?"

Carl gave a noncommittal sigh. His gaze cut to his attorney. The older man stood and pulled on his coat jacket. "Come on, Carl. You've said enough. We'll discuss this more after your arraignment and bail is set."

Patrick waited, giving Carl time to comment and set the record straight. He didn't.

Heading to his office, Patrick bit back a groan. His hope for a break in Amber's case had been overly optimistic. Even before Carl's pathetic confession, Patrick had been getting uneasy vibes.

Carl had never been the cunning one or the brains behind any clash in high school. He was a follower. Muscle when needed. And by his own confession, a drug dealer now. He was careless, reckless. But was he a killer? And if he was, he wouldn't be acting alone.

"Patrick."

Hearing Vance's deep voice, Patrick stopped short and waited for his boss to catch up to him.

Vance gave him a pat on the shoulder. "Good job. I watched your interrogation on the video monitor. You really pulled the information from Shaw. Even with his attorney present."

"Thanks. But it wasn't exactly the information I'd hoped for."

"No, but selling heroin? Who would have thought? People never cease to amaze me."

"Yeah. Handy, isn't it? A popular high school coach moonlighting as a drug dealer." Patrick shook his head. "Consider the customers he had at his fingertips."

"Unfortunate." Vance snickered. "But even if his attorney gets a bail bond for him today, this felony isn't going away. He'll do time. In the meantime, what are you thinking his ties are to Amber's case?"

Patrick inhaled, trying to stay calm, although sitting on the razor-sharp edge of frustration. While Carl stayed mum, Amber's life was on the line. "I don't know how much Carl is involved, but my gut tells me there's someone else, someone shrewder, more devious behind this. And Carl knows who that is."

* * *

Gus's Diner, known for its Southern cuisine and friendly service, was a mom-and-pop establishment close to the police station. Patrick bragged that they made the best comfort food around. And right now comfort of any kind sounded good to Amber.

The decor inside the diner was rustic, but tasteful, with dark, distressed wood-plank floors, lots of wood beams and a large stone fireplace in the center of the dining area. Crisp white linens graced the tables and local artist paintings dotted the walls. The place was packed. The tantalizing aroma of home cooking wafting in the air told her why.

Amber's stomach growled. The appetite she'd lost while waiting for Patrick suddenly returned.

"Table for two—Wiley."

The waitress showed them to a table by the window.

After a cursory glance at the menu, Patrick set his down while Amber continued to peruse hers. So many options. After narrowing down her selections, she peeked over at Patrick.

He was seated back in the chair with his arms firmly folded across his chest. She recognized the encompassing sweep of his eyes as he took in the room. So very cop-like. She couldn't stop a smile. He just couldn't help himself.

That was another quality she loved…liked about him. She picked up her water, took a drink.

"So what did you decide on?"

Unease prickled her skin as he turned his dark, assessing gaze on her. "Some kind of seafood, I think."

"Good choice. They have some great shrimp dishes."

She glanced at the menu again. "Broiled shrimp with creamed spinach and black beans does sound good." Her grumbling stomach agreed.

Patrick gave a wry chuckle. "I was thinking more like

fried Bayou shrimp and mac and cheese. But you always did like veggies on everything. Pizza, subs—"

"—salads." She smiled.

"Yep. Piled high, if I recall."

She nodded. "And I suppose beef is still high on your list of food staples."

"Oh, yeah." He held up a hand a couple inches over his height. "Real high. Unbeknownst to Popeye, red meat is what builds muscles." His smile was teasing, but his words held some truth—that was, if his powerfully muscled physique was any indication.

She breathed a silent sigh.

After the waitress took their orders, Amber started to unwind some and Patrick appeared more relaxed than he'd been an hour ago, after he'd finished talking to Carl. Interrogation had to be stressful, even more so when he didn't get the answers he wanted.

Patrick rested his elbows on the arms of the chair. "So how's your family been? I heard your brother's living somewhere in South America."

He heard about her brother? She wondered if he'd heard anything about her, too. Or maybe he'd avoided topics that involved her, like she had about him? Amber twirled the straw in her drink, making the ice clink. "Jason and his family live in a small village on the coast of Chile. He runs a mission there. Actually, my parents are down there now and will be working with him for the next couple months."

"That's great. I'm sure they're making quite an impact."

"They are." She nodded. "How about your family?"

"Well, my big sister is working on her third master's degree. Communication or information technology something or other." After a slight pause he chuckled. "And she still hasn't decided on a career path."

"Tori must really like school." Amber couldn't imagine. One master's degree was plenty for her. "And your parents—are they doing okay?"

Patrick nodded his head. "My dad's semiretired from the post office. And my mom started working at the day care at church. With no grandkids in the foreseeable future, or maybe never, she's finally getting her baby fix by being a surrogate grandma."

Never? Amber was still processing that statement when Patrick added, "She actually asked about you a couple days ago. She's been keeping up with your situation thanks to the local media."

Amber's face heated and her stomach quivered at the memory of how disappointed Tina Wiley had been after she and Patrick had broken up. Tina had been good friends with Amber's mother, but now they didn't even speak. So many lives had been affected by her one mistake.

Amber swallowed hard, trying not to dwell on the past. "That's nice," she uttered, not really sure how to respond to his mother's renewed interest in her, or to the newspaper's generous coverage of the latest perils in her life.

Patrick sat back against the wood chair. "*Nice* will be when there's nothing left for the paper to report." Though his tone was almost joking, worry darkened his eyes, and her heart stalled in her chest.

She gave a gentle nod. The character of this man was incredible. Instead of scorn, he genuinely cared about her, about her safety, making not falling back in love with him that much harder. For fleeting moments she imagined with more clarity than logic that one day there might be a future for them.

Fortunately she had enough common sense to understand what her heart refused to accept. The only thing on Patrick's agenda that involved her was cracking this case. Then it was back to life as usual, for the both of them.

Shaking off a sense of foreboding, she tore her gaze

away and glanced back at the menu, concentrating on something worth thinking about. "So what would you recommend for dessert?"

She needed comfort food of the best kind.

A short time later, Amber sat back in her seat, completely full and satisfied. The food was delicious and the company…wonderful. She swallowed a sigh.

The topic of the death threats against her hadn't even come up.

"All finished?" The waitress dropped the check folder on the table and gestured to Amber's half-eaten dessert. The hot fudge sundae cake was awesome, but she was stuffed.

"Yes." Amber nodded, rummaging through her purse.

Patrick took out his wallet and, ignoring Amber's objection, handed the waitress his credit card.

"Patrick, you don't have to do that."

"My pleasure. Besides, I owe you one for breakfast."

A warm feeling washed through her. No small deed went unappreciated by him. Although, he owed her nothing.

On their way out the door, the waitress caught up with them. "Miss, I think you dropped this." She handed Amber a rather crumpled copy of one of her fund-raiser brochures.

Amber hiked the strap of her purse higher on her shoulder. You'd think she'd learn to keep her bag zipped. "Thank you."

"Hey, let me see that," Patrick said as she started to stuff it into her bag.

"It's just one of my fund-raiser brochures." She held it up for him to see.

She blinked in surprise when he snatched it out of her hand, his mouth pulling into a grimace.

"Patrick?"

He shook his head, worry shadowing his face.

Amber scrambled beside him. "Oh, my…" She gasped, her heart beating a frantic rhythm as she glanced at the paper in his hand. The title of the fund-raiser, Silence No More, had been crossed out and in its place was scribbled No More Silence Equals Death.

A sick feeling settled like a rock in Amber's stomach. Not only did some crazy man want her dead, but he was also getting close enough to tamper with her things.

TEN

The next morning, Amber poured herself a second cup of coffee and stared out the window above the sink to Kim's small front lawn shimmering in the morning sunshine. The trees were starting to bud, and spring bulbs poked through the brown mulch in the flower beds by the cobblestone walk. Another week and daffodils and tulips would be abundant.

She raised her cup, savoring the hazelnut scent as she took a sip. Spring had finally arrived. Warmth and sunshine. Brilliant colors. Her favorite time of year.

Well, maybe not this year.

Instead, a deeper distress joined the anxiety twisting away at her insides. Not merely because she was on someone's hit list, or at the prospect of finding the identity of her attacker, not even the stress of having Patrick back in her life, but the recent news they'd heard from the forensics team last night. The police had finished their investigation of the attack made on her counseling center.

Now it was time to assess the damage.

The day of the attack she'd been whisked out of the building by officers so quickly she hadn't gotten a good look around. Today was the first day she was allowed back on the property. She couldn't wait to get there.

Patrick, on the other hand, seemed to be in no hurry.

After breakfast he remained at the kitchen table, nursing a cup of coffee and checking emails on his phone. Kim had already left for work. And with her laptop, client notes and files in the messenger bag buried somewhere amid the glass rubble at the center, she had nothing to do except wait.

On a sigh, Amber sought refuge in her cup of coffee. Patrick had a crime to solve. Of course he had more on his mind than Safe Harbor Counseling Center.

Still, she wanted it back up and running again very soon.

How long would it take? She swallowed the last of her drink, rinsed out her coffee cup and then loaded it into the dishwasher. Days? Weeks? Disappointment puddled in her stomach. She still couldn't believe someone had shot up the building. She shut the dishwasher and wiped her hands on a dish towel.

"Are you ready to go?"

Patrick's voice pulled her back to the present and brought her around sharply. She tossed the dish towel on the countertop. "Absolutely." She took off across the kitchen, brushing past him in pursuit of her jacket.

"I just received a message from Vance stating the landlord had the front of the building boarded up. However, the inside will be in the same disarray as when we left. Pretty rough condition. You sure you want to see it like that?" Just by Patrick's tone, she could imagine the concern in his eyes.

"I'll be fine." She put on her jacket. "Besides, Tony emailed me this morning. He wants to stop by also to take a look around and pick up a few things from his office. I told him I'd text him when we're on the way."

Twenty minutes later, ignoring the no-parking zone, Patrick rolled his SUV to a stop outside Safe Harbor Counseling Center. Amber climbed out of the truck and stood outside the yellow police crime tape on the edge of the sidewalk. Her stomach did a little twist as she took in the shell-pocked siding and boarded-up window. Even the sign by the door was riddled with bullet holes. She remembered the rush of pride she felt the day that sign had gone up, the finishing touch to a dream come true.

"You sure you're okay?" Patrick came up beside her.

She nodded. "Yes." Like it or not, she had to be.

As they leaned under the police tape, she mentally prepared herself for what she would find.

Two steps inside, she halted and tried to keep from gasping as Patrick stepped past her and ventured into the thick of the damage. She couldn't believe the destruction before her. There was broken glass everywhere. The floor and the tables, even the top of the lone framed picture still hanging on the wall. The beautiful overstuffed sofa and chair that she'd special ordered and waited five months to get was riddled with bullet holes, and even her favorite potted plant lay amid the rubble.

Overwhelmed by the sight, Amber took a step back, her heart knocking against her ribs. She worked to regulate her breathing. This whole incident only added to the edginess she'd been experiencing since the car bombing. Her nerves were about shot, frazzled from bouncing between fearing for her life and wallowing in the regret of what had gotten her to this point in the first place.

Today something else welled up inside her: a surge of defensive anger. Nobody deserved to be a victim of somebody's hate. Someone so sinister and unwilling to comprehend the lasting destruction of their actions.

This emotional response was new, although a concept she firmly believed in and reinforced in her clients. After years of blaming herself and even God for what had happened to her, she was ready to accept that truth for herself. She wasn't to blame for the vicious choice someone else had made.

Amber took an elongated breath, filling her lungs and reveling for a moment in an odd sense of peace. Maybe she was starting to heal?

"Wow, this is a disaster."

She turned enough to see Tony grimace as he hovered in the doorway. His statement summed up the situation perfectly. "It is amazing how destructive a few little bullets could be."

"Few? It looks as though the building got hosed by a machine gun."

"A military-style semiautomatic assault rifle, actually." Patrick stepped back through the rubble with her leather messenger bag in his hand. "It's not as powerful as a machine gun, but it can spray large areas with a hail of bullets."

Tony gave a slow whistle. "That it did."

Amber's heart pinched. This was what the men and women who served in the armed forces were up against. She gained a new appreciation for them and for Patrick. He'd risked his life for his country, and now he was doing so again for her.

"I believe this is yours." Patrick handed her the messenger bag.

"Thank you." She took it from him, feeling a bit of relief. At least she could get some work done now.

"If you'll excuse me…" Tony stepped carefully around the glass rubble. "I need to grab a few things in my office."

Patrick moved aside, allowing him to pass by.

As Tony headed down the hallway, he glanced back. "Do you need me to get anything of yours, Amber?"

"No, but thank you." Amber shook her head. "I have my laptop and notes. I should be fine."

"All right."

Well, maybe *fine* wasn't the right word. Amber turned her attention to Patrick and motioned to the mess around them. "Can you believe all this damage?"

"I've seen worse." Patrick stood with his hands on his hips, his gaze skimming the area.

Of course, things could be worse. She needed to hold on to that perspective.

The structure itself, part of a run of historical buildings, had survived hurricanes, tornados and fires over the years. Safe Harbor would survive, she assured herself. "I hope it won't take long to make repairs."

"It shouldn't. We'll get a crime scene cleanup crew in. And once things settle down you can meet up with the landlord and get things going."

Confused, Amber looked from the gunfire rubble to Patrick. "Once things settle down? I'd like to get started immediately. I need to get back to work."

"Amber." Small frown lines rippled across his forehead and he narrowed his eyes. "I wanted to talk to you about this after we left today, but I'll mention it now. I'd like to get you set up in a safe house. An undisclosed location where there is round-the-clock security."

"A safe house?" Amber straightened, already disliking the idea. "Clues are coming in. Randall and Carl are being watched. Patrol cars are monitoring Kim's neighborhood and you haven't left my side..." Her words petered out as a revelation exploded in her mind. Of course, he had to be tired of hanging around. He had a personal life he'd been neglecting.

"Amber, listen—"

"No, Patrick." She held up a hand. "I know you're a busy man. I can't expect for you to stand guard over me. I can't afford to pay for security on my own, but I can talk to my parents."

"That's not what I'm trying to say." He put both hands

on her shoulders, holding her gaze and sending a shiver down the length of her arms. "I just want you to be safe. I can't make you go to the safe house, but just think about it. Once we get this case figured out, you can go back to life as usual."

She heard the words, but they didn't truly register in her mind. She was too affected by the heat of his touch. A sizzling warmth she'd not felt since the last time he'd touched her. She swallowed again and tried hard to rein in her thoughts. She couldn't let this man get to her.

"...a short hiatus won't kill you. Being distracted and not watching your back just might."

"A hiatus?" Amber blinked and inched back, out of his grasp, her thoughts finally kicking in. "But I have the fund-raiser to plan. A business to run."

"You can still work while you're at the safe house."

"What about Pam and Tony? And my clients?"

"Pam and Tony can work from home. And your clients, well...this is a temporary situation." Patrick leaned closer, his gleaming brown eyes holding traces of concern. "This guy is getting bolder. Who knows what desperate plan he has next? In fact, if we aren't any closer to finding him by next week, you should postpone the fund-raiser."

She deflated like a leaky balloon. "That is exactly what that creep wants, for me to give up and run into hiding. If there's no fund-raiser, his concerns are alleviated about me telling my story as part of my keynote speech."

"Fear of you going public may indeed be his motivator, however, he also wants you dead. That's the part I'm wor—" Patrick halted midsentence when the ringtone sounded on his phone. He pressed it to his ear. "This is Patrick Wiley."

Amber brushed back a wisp of hair with shaky fingers, quietly rejoicing at the distraction. If she had to, she'd hire more security, but no way was she giving in to her assailant. Whether his identity was known or not, or even if the fund-raiser had to be postponed, she planned to tell her story. To publically encourage women not to hang on to the guilt and shame of abuse—like she had.

Tears blurred her eyes. Blinking to clear them, a sense of freedom washed through her.

Closure. She breathed. That was what she needed.

"Patrick is right, Amber." Tony stepped toward her, glass crunching beneath his boots. "I overheard what he said about the fund-raiser, and like I mentioned before, it might be a good idea to just postpone it."

"That topic isn't up for discussion," she snapped a little too quickly. She hated to sound unreasonable, but she wasn't ready to give up yet. Surely by next week this whole nightmare would be behind her.

"Okay." Tony waved his hand with dismissal. "Your call. But keep it in mind."

"I will." She nodded, softening her inflection. "I just think the fund-raiser is important, both for the community and for me."

"For you?" Tony raised an eyebrow. "You're not still considering sharing your story, are you? Not with all this nonsense going on."

There was a moment's hesitation as Amber swallowed around the lump lodged in her throat. "I think it's time."

"When and where?" The spike in Patrick's tone made her shift focus.

Wheeling around toward him, she noticed the muscles in his jaw clench as he wound up the call. "I'll meet you there in an hour." He pocketed his phone, his eyes darkened, narrowed on her. "That was Carl Shaw. I'm meeting him at a bar and grill south of here at noon."

Amber's heart stopped. She glanced at Tony, who was following the conversation with wide eyes.

"Sounds as though something's about to go down."

Tony gave an impressive arch of his brow and a thumbs-up. "Keep me posted, Amber." He tucked his laptop case under his arm and headed out the door.

"All right." She breathed deep, hoping this was the break they needed. She turned back to Patrick. "Did he give you any indication if he was going to confess? Or just give you information?"

"Nope. He didn't specify." He cupped her elbow, shepherding her toward the exit. "But whatever information he has is sure to help us." Optimism rang in his tone.

And in her heart.

After dropping Amber off at the station house, Patrick punched the gas and headed toward Moe's Grille, a hole-in-the-wall restaurant located in one of the low-rent districts on the outskirts of Savannah. When he'd suggested for Amber to hang out in his office while he was gone, first she balked at the idea. He couldn't think of a safer place, and didn't have time to come up with a better alternative. He wondered if she truly understood the danger she was in.

Patrick didn't even bother to ponder that question. He kept a steady hand on the steering wheel and pulled onto the highway ramp. The radio dispatcher had reported an earlier accident with cars backed up for five miles. To his relief, traffic flowed steadily on both sides of the thoroughfare. The last thing he wanted was to keep Carl waiting.

Seventeen miles down the road, he took the exit for Tallwater Boulevard, a four-lane street on the neighborhood's main drag.

Patrick pulled into a public parking lot two buildings down from Moe's Grille and checked the clock on the dash. Noon. Right on time. He slowly maneuvered his SUV through the tight rows of cars and scanned the lot for the yellow pickup Carl had said he'd be driving.

He could see why Carl had picked this place, a popular

local restaurant off the beaten path. It was easier not to be noticed in a crowd. Carl Shaw was afraid of something, and Patrick was itching to hear what that *something* was.

After he took a second loop around the lot, Patrick's heart sank a bit when he didn't see the yellow truck. He hoped Shaw hadn't chickened out.

He pulled around to the rear of the lot and backed into an open parking space.

Minutes ticked by. Drumming his fingers on the center console, he took in the area while still keeping an eye out for Carl. Directly behind him were an old feed store, barely standing, and a two-pump gas station. To his right, a couple of decrepit storage buildings, some ancient rusty oil tanks and overgrown vegetation. A deserted office building stood in front of him, and to his left, across the street, a Laundromat and several more locally owned diners.

Finally a yellow dual-cab pickup pulled into the rear entrance of the parking lot.

Patrick was just about to climb out of his SUV when he heard a loud *pop, pop, pop.*

His heart pounding, he kicked open the driver's-side door and dropped to his feet, weapon ready. Staying low, he moved to the front bumper, stretched to look over the hood. Swiftly, he gave the parking lot another encompassing glance, looking for the shooter or anything suspicious.

Nothing moved, except Carl's truck, which was now weaving out of control. After sideswiping a parked vehicle, it spun and skidded several yards into a metal gate marked No Trespassing. The gate flew off. The truck jolted right, then left before slamming head-on into an old oak tree.

Patrick grabbed his cell phone and called for backup. Then he rolled into action and raced toward the accident, gun drawn and his eyes peeled.

A siren blared in the distance within moments.

Smoke spilled from the buckled hood. Looking inside,

Patrick saw Carl's body slumped over the steering wheel. Blood was oozing from a wound on the side of his head. He yanked open the door, and felt for a pulse.

There wasn't one.

ELEVEN

Judging from the troubled expression on Patrick's face when he walked in the office, Amber didn't expect good news. Now the burning question in her mind was, if his talk with Carl hadn't produced any new clues or evidence, where did they go next? More than ever she needed this thing over with. The last thing she wanted was to end up in a safe house.

"Sorry it took so long." He sounded a bit harried. Maybe she was wrong. Maybe Carl did supply him with some intriguing information he needed to jump on.

"I was beginning to wonder." She smiled at him.

He didn't seem to notice, clearly distracted. She volleyed back to her original assumption that things hadn't gone well with Carl. "Hopefully you weren't too bored," he said, pulling off his jacket and tossing it on the back of the file-laden chair beside her.

Since it was a statement, not a question, she didn't even respond. He looked as if he had more on his mind than worrying about her being cooped up in his office with nothing to do but hope for good news while his desk phone rang off the hook.

Now it rang again.

Patrick walked around his desk to answer it.

Reluctantly, Amber sank onto the edge of a chair, trying to ward off any speculation. At the same time she held on to a thread of hope that Carl had supplied Patrick with some tidbit of information that would help crack the case.

"There's definitely a drug tie to this, has to be," Patrick said into the phone. He shoved his hand through his hair, making it stand up in short spikes, before he combed it back down with his fingers.

She tried not to eavesdrop, but her ears perked up when he said, "Find out everything you can on Carl Shaw. Who he partied with. The name of his drug dealer. Old friends. New friends. Anything. And find out if he still had ties to Randall Becker." Patrick hung up the phone and met Amber's gaze. "Sorry, I meant to call you with an update sooner, but I've been on the phone for the past hour."

Shifting uncomfortably, she shrugged. "No problem. Doesn't sound as though you had a very productive meeting with Carl."

"Carl's dead."

Her jaw fell slack. Thank goodness she was sitting down. "What? I mean, how?"

"Someone shot him in the head as he drove into the parking lot at Moe's."

A dead weight settled in her stomach, along with the knowledge that this crime was more complicated than she'd ever imagined. She brushed a strand of hair from her face. "And the shooter?"

Patrick lifted his hands in exasperation. "Don't know."

"This is crazy."

"Yes, it is." Patrick rocked back in his chair with a sigh. "To make matters worse, the ballistics reports came back on the bullets recovered from the attack on the counseling center. None of the bullets matched any of the guns registered to Carl." As he spoke, the frustration in his voice grew thicker.

He always seemed so strong, so in control. A cool self-assurance that encouraged her and kept her grounded. She'd forgotten how just having him in the same room made her feel safe. She didn't like this change in demeanor.

Amber drew in a calming breath, digging deep for composure. "How many people are involved in this?" She almost hated to ask.

There was a flicker of hesitation.

She straightened and caught Patrick's eye. He quirked a brow and sighed. "That's the question of the day."

"So where does the investigation go from here?"

"We'll start dissecting the lives of every guy at that frat party. But still keep Randall Becker at the forefront of our investigation. I just put a tail on him."

Alarm sent tiny pinpricks of fear hopscotching up her spine. "And if Randall isn't the one?"

He shrugged. "We'll keep looking."

Amber slumped back in her chair, her mind trying to sort through the new information. As it started to sink in, she came back up in her seat. "With Carl dead and Randall under surveillance, I'd like to hang out at Kim's house awhile longer. I'm not comfortable with the safe house idea." She held her breath, waited for him to respond.

Patrick gave her an arched look. "I don't think staying at Kim's is wise." Then, as if he could read her thoughts, he rocked forward and his eyes latched firmly on to hers. "And it's not because I'm tired of hanging around you."

"Thank you. I appreciate that," she said, downplaying her earlier concern. Suddenly embarrassed under his penetrating glare, she added, "I didn't want you to feel obligated to spend all your free time protecting me."

Patrick wagged his head. "My job is to solve this case. I'm one hundred percent invested until that happens."

Of course. Her heart slipped a little. "Well, if it's okay with you, I'd like to hold off a few more days before I am sequestered anywhere."

He scratched his jaw. "You're still holding out on the fund-raiser?"

She chewed her bottom lip and nodded.

"But if we're at an impasse in a few more days—"

"I'll gladly go."

"Okay." He stood. "If the safe house is out for now, then let's have some lunch."

Amber was out of the chair and pulling on her jacket before he had a chance to change his thinking. "Sounds good. I'm starving."

The long day turned into an even longer evening.

In Kim's living room, Amber shifted against the arm of the sofa and adjusted her computer on her lap. Scrolling down the screen, she read over the rough draft of the speech she'd been working on.

With an inward cringe, she hit the delete key and erased it all. Closing her eyes, she inhaled slowly, digging deep for inspiration.

A few thoughts came to mind and she started typing again. The words flowed freely, quickly beneath her fingertips. Several sentences later, she read over what she'd written, hope soaring that she was on to something.

She bit her lip. Not quite. *Rough draft* was way too generous of a description. She hit Delete.

Following that routine, she worked for the next couple of hours. She only completed two paragraphs. And they weren't great.

Amber sagged back into the depths of the sofa, pressing her fingertips against her throbbing temples. Even her brain was tired.

Kim, occupying the opposite end of the sofa, passed her a fleeting smile before refocusing on her ebook reader. Across from them, Patrick rested with his feet up and crossed in the recliner as he studied the computer tablet in his hands.

Seeing them actually startled her for a moment. She'd almost forgotten she wasn't alone. The room was ridiculously quiet for being occupied by three people. Of course, all were caught in an electronic fog.

Ah, the digital age.

She laughed inside, not daring to break the sacred silence.

Patrick cleared his throat, doing it for her.

Good, she was still among humans. She smiled this time and looked back at the disjointed speech on her computer screen. She sobered. She'd hardly written a fluid thought. Even with a clear topic, speech writing was harder than she envisioned. Then again, why should she bother to even write out her speech? She knew all too well what she needed to say.

Amber shut her laptop with a snap.

Patrick looked up. "How's the speech coming?"

"I'm finished." She smiled. "What about you? Any breaking news across the wire?"

Patrick lowered the foot of the recliner. "As a matter of fact, I was just going through the data Liza sent. She found out that Carl ran in a marathon a couple months ago. And on the 5K roster, it listed Randall Becker as his running partner."

Amber wrapped her mind around that tidbit. "So Carl and Randall were still friends?"

"So it seems, although they both denied it." Patrick got to his feet, stretched a little. "We're still matching puzzle pieces, but Randall's name keeps popping up as the right fit. I have a feeling his days as a free man are numbered. I plan to see Liza tomorrow morning. I'll see what else she came up with that might help us tie him to this case."

Liza. The pain behind Amber's temples thumped harder.

She had no right feeling jealous. She didn't even know if Patrick had a relationship with that cute little blonde—

Okay. Enough speculation. Patrick deserved a nice, beautiful woman in his life. Eleven years ago she'd made choices she needed to accept, as well as the consequences. And accepting that reality kept her on track.

Amber drew a deep breath and stood. "Tea, anyone?"

Patrick didn't hesitate. "Sure."

"None for me." Kim closed her ereader and yawned. "I'm exhausted, and six o'clock will be here before I know it."

"You sure? Not even a cup of chamomile?"

"No, thanks." Kim was up and already trudging toward her bedroom. "Who would have believed I'd ever be eager to jump into bed by eight-thirty? Ah, the perils of being a nurse."

Amber exchanged an amused smile with Patrick.

She knew what her friend was up to. No matter how much Amber reminded her that having Patrick on her case was awkward at best, whenever there was free time to mingle, Kim made herself scarce, giving her and Patrick more time alone. As if being with him all day wasn't enough.

Amber shoved her laptop into its carrying case as Patrick stood at the arm of the sofa, waiting. "I guess we're on our own," she said, nonplussed by Kim's assumption that something would rekindle between them. After so long and all the grief she'd caused him, that wasn't going to happen. Her romance-minded friend was wasting her matchmaking skills on them.

Even as Amber thought the words, her heart crimped. She should never use *romance* and *Patrick* in the same sentence. "Okay. Let's have some tea." She rose from her seat.

"All right." Patrick gestured for her to go first.

She made her way into the kitchen, Patrick right behind her.

Stretching on tiptoes, she pulled a box of tea from the cabinet, the one she'd bought Kim for Christmas. "Your choices are chamomile, Sleepytime, raspberry, blueberry, peppermint, peach, licorice spice, chai—"

"Hold on." Patrick laughed. "How many varieties are in that box?"

"Just one more. Lavender."

He cocked an eyebrow, doubt in his eyes. "You can drink lavender?"

"Absolutely. Do you want to try some?"

"If you're sure it won't kill me."

"Actually it's good for you. It aids in indigestion, insomnia, headaches, things like that."

"Perfect. I've got all three." Patrick settled into a seat at the table.

Amber smiled, understanding completely. She filled the kettle and put it to boil on the stove. "So about tomorrow, I'd like to see my clients at the women's shelter. And, if possible, run by the banquet hall to make sure everything is in order for next week."

Her remark was met by silence.

Amber glanced over her shoulder and found him staring off, his lips pulled into a straight line, his brow scrunched tight.

She probably didn't want to know what he was thinking about.

Several more seconds beat between them. Had he even heard her?

She swung around and leaned her hip against the cabinet, waiting. He plucked a small notepad from his pocket and jotted something down. "Patrick?"

His gaze swung to hers. "Yes?"

"I just wanted to make sure you heard me." She grabbed two mugs from the cabinet, plopped a tea bag in each.

"I heard you. I'm trying to run through my plans for

tomorrow and figure out how to get you where you need to be." That infamous brow lift was back. "And keep you safe in the process."

Relief trickled through her. "I could drive myself, maybe ask Tony or Pam to tag along."

"Nope, too risky."

The shrill whistle of the teakettle made Amber jump. She turned off the stove and filled the mugs with hot water. "Maybe I could ask one of them to drive me?"

"Neither Tony nor Pam offers you any protection, and you'll be putting them in danger."

"Right." She carried the steaming mugs to the table.

Patrick took the one she offered him. "I'll drop you off at the center in the morning and you can stay for the day. The building is equipped with security cameras, and I'll arrange for an officer to patrol the area. And keep your smartphone with you."

"Okay."

Patrick stirred a packet of sugar into his tea. "Then around four o'clock I can pick you up and take you down to the community center."

This man was amazing. Too amazing. Guilt tightened her gut. After all she'd put him through, he was still willing to do this for her. She tried to think of something fitting to say to make him understand how much she appreciated his help. Something that wouldn't involve dredging up the past to make her point.

She settled on a simple "Thank you" and took the seat beside him.

Patrick set his teaspoon down with a clank and picked up his mug. He cleared his voice lightly. "So, Amber, tell me—what do you do for fun these days?"

For a moment she was caught off guard. Was this a detective question? Or was Patrick Wiley just curious? "Like a hobby?"

"Yeah, a hobby." Patrick lifted his cup and took a sip and then said, "Or anything you do for fun."

Which would be… Amber paused, racking her brain. Work and more work didn't sound like a hobby or particularly fun in the scheme of leisure activities. Then she remembered the spring plants she'd just purchased.

"I like to garden."

"Garden, as in vegetables?"

"Not vegetables. Herbs, flowers—"

"Lavender?" He laughed between sips. "Hey. This isn't bad."

A sudden warmth curled around Amber. She loved the way he laughed. The way he smiled. The way— *Whoa.* She shifted in her seat. *Enough of that.* She took a long, slow breath. "I'm glad you like your tea. I haven't tried growing lavender yet. But I have some seedlings in my garage ready to plant…well, assuming they're still alive."

"Hopefully they are." After a short silence he asked, "So what else keeps you busy?"

Amber sipped her tea, wondering where this was going. Was he hoping to engage her in casual conversation and draw new information from her?

Clever tactic. Something she used in counseling herself.

She lowered her cup. "I used to volunteer at church."

Where had that come from? That had been eons ago. She bit her lip, noticing Patrick's assessing brown stare.

"Used to?"

She nodded.

Almost fleetingly a glint of sadness shone in his eyes. "You know, Amber, our faith in God is what sustains us when things get tough."

Her pulse pounded a frantic rhythm. While his faith was bolstered by the trials in his life, her faith remained frayed, so worn away and neglected by the pain of her past. She attempted a smile that failed.

"I hope that truth comes back to you."

"I'm working on it." His words, although soothing, stung all the way to her soul. She hoped for renewed faith, too. Slowly, her heart was starting to heal.

Someday maybe she'd possess the faith she once had.

The parking lot was nearly full when Patrick pulled up to Coastal Karate School. He recognized Randall's Jeep and parked right next to it.

He walked inside the dojo and looked around. Through several windows he saw classes in session, and otherwise not a soul in sight. Patrick stood there a moment, mulling over his choices, whether to wait it out until classes ended or start knocking on doors.

"Sir, may I help you?" A young man, looking to be in his late teens and dressed in a white martial arts uniform with a brown belt, came out of one of the classrooms.

Problem solved. Patrick lifted his chin. "I'm looking for Randall Becker."

The young man strode toward him. "He's teaching a class right now. I'm Kyle, one of his assistants. Maybe I can help?"

"I don't think so." Patrick pulled out his badge. "I hate to interrupt Mr. Becker's class, but I need to speak to him. Is that possible?"

Kyle's head bobbed up and down. "Yes, sir. I'll get him."

Two minutes later, Randall walked out of a room. He was dressed in the same martial arts gear as his assistant, but he wore a black belt that slapped at his thighs as he stormed toward Patrick. He was wound way too tight for someone with nothing to hide. "What are you doing here, Wiley?"

"Well, good afternoon to you, too, Randall."

Randall snorted, halting three feet from Patrick.

Patrick crossed his arms, met Randall's stare. "Actually, I need to ask you a few more questions."

"I answered more than enough questions the last time you were here."

"Well, I have a couple more. Do you want to talk someplace private?"

Randall shoved his fists on his hips and glanced around before taking a step closer to Patrick. "You've got nothing on me, Wiley." His voice was low, but his tone was lethal.

Patrick stood for a moment eyeing Randall's defensive stance. He wasn't about to lose his cool, although it wasn't easy to maintain control. What he wouldn't give for a little sparring practice with black belt Randall. Not that he'd hurt the guy. Just maybe knock him down a few pegs. "The last time I was here, Randall, you denied being friends with Carl Shaw. Yet the roster for the 5K you ran just a few months back listed him as your running partner."

"So?" Annoyance stamped his face.

"Lying to a law enforcement officer is never a good idea."

Randall jutted a thick finger at him. "It's none of your business who my friends are. Or were." He paused, cleared his voice. "Like I said, Wiley. You've got nothing on me."

"I'd like you to come down to the precinct with me and tell us what you know about Carl. You're not under arrest, but I think it would be in your best interest."

Randall leaned in and whispered through clenched teeth, "Calling my attorney is in my best interest. Once again, Wiley, you can't tie me to anything."

Patrick shifted his weight and mimicked Randall's rigid stance. "Because you're not guilty? Or because you're good at hiding something?"

"I'm done talking to you." His voice turned to ice now.

Patrick pressed on. "Where were you yesterday around noon?"

His entire face twisted and he practically growled, "You sure don't do your homework, do you, Wiley?"

"And what homework would that be?" Patrick asked with growing impatience.

Patrick waited as Randall panned the area, his head swiveling left and then right. Satisfied that they were alone, his lips curled into a smirk. "I spent the day in jail, bozo."

"Jail?" Patrick crossed his arms, showing no outward sign of his astonishment. Too bad he hadn't put a tail on him sooner.

"Yeah." Randall droned on. "Stopped by my own house to pick up a few things yesterday morning, and my soon-to-be ex-wife called the cops. Said she felt threatened, imagine that?"

Patrick didn't respond to that. Instead, he said, "Why don't you tell me what you know about Carl."

Randall moved slightly closer. "The only thing I have to say to you is this—I want you out of my building. And if you ever come back, be prepared for a little one-to-one with me. I've got a training room ready."

So the man could read his mind. Patrick grinned. "I hope I can take you up on that one day."

"Good, because there's nothing I wouldn't love more than to grind your face into the mat." Randall turned and stomped away.

And Patrick would love to give him the chance to try.

TWELVE

Amber strode down the hallway at the Savannah Battered Women's Shelter and headed toward the last office on the left. The place was bustling. Had been all day. Besides the scheduled group meetings on life and parenting skills led by the case workers and counselors, local church volunteers had stopped by to stock the food pantry and give haircuts to the women and children.

Much of Amber's day was spent meeting with individual patrons, offering counsel and working on plans to get them back on their feet. Not an easy assignment given the limited community resources in the area.

Still, the normalcy of the activity put Amber at ease. Dealing with the problems of others kept her from dwelling on her own.

Amber poked her head into the office of the shelter director, Christine Carmichael. "Thanks, Christine, for letting me hang out with you guys today."

Christine's fingers paused over her keyboard. She looked up with a smile. "You're always welcome here, Amber, you know that. Our space may be at a minimum, but I'll make sure there's always an office open for you."

"Thank you." Amber returned the smile, grateful for the offer but also hopeful her center would be up and running before long. "I need to make a couple of copies. Do you mind if I grab some paper from the supply room? The printer across the hall is out."

"Help yourself."

"Thank you. I'll be leaving after that. So I'll see you next week."

"All right." Christine nodded. "Be safe out there."

Safety. A looming issue Amber didn't want to be reminded of. "I will." She hoped so anyway. She swallowed a sigh.

In the basement Amber scanned the jumbled rows of shelves, freshly stocked with boxes of pens, markers, notepads, file folders and…ah, copy paper.

On tiptoes she reached to the fifth shelf as a hollow *thump* broke the silence.

A chill prickled her skin.

Daring not to move, not breathe, she waited a moment, listened. Another series of swift taps. One. Two. Three. The muffled, rhythmic beats sounded like soft footsteps.

Panic set in. Amber spun to the doorway, peeked around the corner. She saw nothing. She held her breath. The eerie beat eroded into a dull whir as the air conditioner cycled on.

Only the air conditioner. Amber exhaled, smiling at her overactive imagination. The shelter had round-the-clock security, cameras and alarms. No one could get in.

She spun back, and as she grabbed a ream of copy paper she heard a scuffling sound, followed by shuffling footfalls. Louder. Creeping closer.

The thud of the paper hitting the ground momentarily drowned out the squeak of footsteps. Her nerves flared.

"Who's there?" she shouted, fear choking her.

No answer came.

Forgoing the copy paper, Amber wheeled around, headed for the door. At the doorway, she quickly glanced into the corridor, feeling a smidgen better when she saw no one. But then there was a click and everything went black.

An overwhelming dread surged through her—it was petrifying, oppressive. The feeling stole her breath and thrust her back into that murky frat room. Her heart pounding against her ribs, Amber took off to the right and picked her way down the corridor, avoiding stacks of boxes and old furniture.

A clank, then a loud clatter came from the darkness behind her, as if someone had tripped over something. The footsteps quickened, her heartbeat with them.

Fresh fear spiraled through her, escalating further at the sound of a taunting chuckle.

Fixated on getting out of there, Amber didn't look back, didn't stop, even as her ankle grazed the brick wall at the stairwell. Grabbing the stair rail, she bounded up the metal steps to the top. "Help!" She desperately clawed for the doorknob, finally latching on to it just as the door swung open.

Plunging through the opening, Amber fell onto her knees, her palms smacking against the linoleum. Looking up, she saw Lou, the security guard, and Carol, one of the counselors, staring down at her.

"Miss Amber, are you okay?" Lou asked as he helped her to her feet.

Her eyes darted between the inky darkness behind her and her colleagues. "The lights went off and somebody's down there."

The older gentleman turned wide eyes on Amber. "Was it one of the counselors or a client?"

"I don't know." Amber barely got the words out, she was so out of breath. "No one answered."

Lou nodded, reached around her and flipped on the light switch. "I'll take a look."

"Should you be going down there alone?"

"I've got my radio and Taser right here." He tapped the holster on his belt. "But chances are slim of someone getting in from the outside." He headed into the basement, his heavy work boots clanking down the metal steps.

Amber leaned against the wall, anxiety churning her stomach. "If someone did get in, what if they already got away?"

Carol shook her head, her gaze gentle. "Lou's right, it would be tough for someone to get in…or out, especially without a badge. Somebody probably hit the light switch not realizing you were down there. It's an old building. One switch controls everything."

"But…I heard someone." Amber straightened, panic still cycling through her. "I think we should call the police…or—"

Carol cut her off, eyes narrowing. "Like I said, it's an old building, so there's lots of creaky and eerie noises. If someone had gotten in without a badge, an alarm sounds and the police are instantly notified."

"But I really did—"

Carol held up her hand. "Hold on, let's check with Lou. There aren't many places to hide down there." She stepped to the door, glanced down. "Lou, you okay?"

"Coast is clear," he hollered back. "No one's down here."

Tumultuous thoughts pelted Amber. Maybe paranoia was getting the best of her. Or was she just going crazy? Probably a little of both.

Carol turned back to Amber, rubbed her shoulder. "You've had a lot going on. It's hard not to be paranoid."

Amber attempted a small smile that wasn't quite successful. "Thanks, Carol. I think I'll just download the files to my flash drive and print them out later."

On still-shaky legs, Amber headed into an office down the hall.

She sat down in front of the keyboard, pulled her flash drive from her pocket and connected it to the shelter's computer system. With a flick of the mouse, the screen came to life and she started to download her client files. She should have done this to start with.

"You didn't tell me you'd be here today."

Amber's head snapped up. From the other side of the doorway, Tony's wide grin greeted her. She leaned back in her seat and smiled. "Actually, I wasn't sure until late last night. Patrick doesn't think I should be driving alone, and I feel rather awkward asking him to take me wherever I need to go."

"Next time, give me a call. I'll be happy to give you a ride. I agree with Patrick, you shouldn't be driving alone right now." Tony dragged a straight-back chair from the corner of the room, placed it close to the desk and plunked down into it.

"Thank you." She looped a strand of hair behind her ear. "But with a target on my back, it wouldn't be a good idea for you to drive me, either."

"You're probably right. I guess I'll leave chauffeuring you around to that detective of yours."

She didn't miss his words. *Detective of yours.* She breathed deep, not even wanting to entertain that thought. "Patrick has been great. He rearranged his schedule to drop me off this morning. And this afternoon he agreed to run me by the Port City Community Center to firm up the details for the fund-raiser."

"Your own personal bodyguard. You can't beat that." Tony leaned back in the chair, folded his arms and crossed one ankle over the other. "The ex-boyfriend thing. Is it going okay?"

"Fine...well, awkward, but fine."

That elicited a chuckle. "Sounds interesting."

To say the least, she thought. She nodded her reply.

"So bring me up to speed on what else is going on with the case."

Amber shifted in her chair. "What do you want? The long, drawn-out version, or a quick summary?"

Tony shrugged one shoulder. "Quick summary, I guess."

"A lot of dead ends and cold leads."

He gazed at her, with one eyebrow raised. "There must be something significant."

"*Nada.* Well, except Patrick is certain Carl Shaw was somehow involved. And probably Randall Becker."

"Shaw. He's the one that's—"

"Dead. Yeah."

Tony pulled at the tuft of goatee under his lower lip. "Unbelievable. Whoever this guy is, he seems to stop at nothing."

"The worst part, whoever is trying to kill me wants to protect himself from being discovered. Yet what he doesn't realize is that I have no recollection of who he is."

"Maybe he's afraid that one day your repressed memories will come back."

Amber shook her head. "A delusional fear on his part. I never even saw the guy."

"Ah." Tony lifted his index finger. "But the mind is a funny thing. You never know. Then again, even if you never remember, making your story known would spark speculation that could jog someone else's memory or lead to an investigation, if not by police, then maybe by the media. As you know the media are pretty good about digging up dirt. Somebody who attended that party has something to hide."

"Like Carl?"

Tony shrugged. "Just saying, a lot of folks have secrets they don't want uncovered."

She reluctantly nodded. She hadn't considered that. Nor did she want to. If Tony was on to something, who knew how many people who had attended that party had secrets that were worth killing over.

Inside the department's crime analysis office, Patrick poured himself a cup of coffee as he waited for Liza to finish a phone call. Seated at her desk on the opposite side of the room, she'd been jotting down notes from the time he'd walked in. Hopefully answers to questions about Amber's case. He needed a break, something to jump-start his stalled investigation.

Patrick plopped into a chair with a huge sigh. Crossing one ankle over his knee, he took a swig of the strong brew. Time was of the essence. Ten days until Amber's fund-raiser and he needed not only fresh clues, but also cold hard facts.

Something to tie Randall to Amber's attack and, if his gut was right, to Carl Shaw's murder.

Liza finally hung up the phone and turned to Patrick, her pale blue eyes indicating her exhaustion. She'd been working hard on this case. He appreciated that.

"Any news?" He lifted a brow.

Liza nodded. "It seems that Randall Becker has another hobby besides karate and running 5k marathons."

"And what would that be?"

"Peddling drugs."

Much intrigued, Patrick sat up straighter. "Really?"

The door flew open. Captain Peterson came ambling into the room munching on a cheeseburger. "I thought I'd find you here."

Patrick set his drink down and stood. "What do you know, Vance?"

"The ballistics report came back on the bullet that killed Carl Shaw."

"And?"

"Perfect match to the bullets fired at Amber's center."

Things looked better all the time. "Good news. Liza also found another interesting tidbit about Randall." Patrick gestured toward Liza, prompting her to tell him.

Liza pushed back in her chair. "Two years ago he was arrested for possession of heroin and marijuana with intent to sell. The charges were dropped before he went to court. Within six weeks, he opened his karate school—a three-million-dollar venture."

"Debt-free?" Patrick and Vance both said at the same time.

"Not debt-free. He has a loan with an offshore trust. This all happened about the same time Carl bought his first house. Coincidently, his loan is also with an offshore trust of a different name."

"Find out who the trustees are." Vance jumped on that one.

Liza nodded. "I have someone working on that now."

"There's a lot of banking secrecy in offshore accounts," Patrick said, shaking his head.

"True," Vance said. "Drug cartels and money-laundering schemes are never easy to track."

Patrick whistled softly between his teeth. "So both Carl Shaw and Randall Becker moonlighted as drug dealers…" He stopped, let that soak in, then said, "One or both were concerned about Amber linking them to what happened eleven years ago at a frat party."

"Appears that way." Liza nodded.

Dozens of scenarios blew through Patrick's head, none of which made sense. "If whoever wants Amber out of the picture and thought she knew who he was, why not kill her years ago?"

Vance's mouth was full. He held up a finger while he swallowed. "Maybe she never posed a threat before."

Patrick thought about that. "Okay. I get it. The fundraiser obviously is a threat to somebody. But why assume she would tell her story now, when she'd kept silent for all these years?"

"Especially since she never saw her attacker," Vance added, chucking his wrapper in the trash.

"Maybe it has something to do with her rising notoriety in the community?" Liza offered.

"Maybe," Patrick murmured, thinking back to something Amber had told him. "Amber had kept quiet about what happened and the event basically blew over, no charges filed, no investigation. Now she's coming out of her shell, speaking out against abuse against women."

Liza smiled. "So you may be looking for more than her attacker."

"True. Someone who knew what had taken place that night and has drug ties to Randall and Carl."

"Makes sense." Vance slapped Patrick on the shoulder on his way out the door. "I have a feeling this case is about to blow right open."

Patrick thought so, too.

He turned on his heel and followed Vance out the door. "Thanks, Liza," he called over his shoulder. "You've been a great help. If you find out anything else, let me know."

"There is one more thing, Patrick."

Midstride, Patrick halted, turned back.

Liza stared at him for a moment, twirled a pen in her hand.

Patrick shifted, quirked an eyebrow. "What is it?"

She rested an elbow on the desk. "I did find one more interesting tidbit." Her slender eyebrows pulled slightly together. "It seems Amber Talbot once had a fiancé. She broke their engagement after the frat party incident."

A story he knew well. But the reminder still cut like a knife. "That's correct."

"So sad. One traumatic event changed everything." A beat passed. "Why didn't you tell me, Patrick?"

"That I used to be engaged to Amber?" Patrick shrugged. "If I thought it was relevant to the case, I would have."

"This case is personal to you." She dropped her pen and crossed her arms over her chest. "All the work I've done, and you already knew most of it. I wish I had known I was just filling in the blanks."

"Actually, I knew very little." Patrick raised his hands, palms out, warding off a lecture. "Amber never divulged anything about a frat house party or what had happened until she was attacked at her house."

A frown tightened Liza's brow further. "Are you talking about her attack a few days ago?"

"I am." Patrick nodded.

"Eleven years after the frat party incident?"

"Unfortunately." It was a fact he wasn't proud of.

Her eyes narrowed. "Seems odd that she wouldn't share something so traumatic with you."

Guilt swelled Patrick's chest, but he didn't let it show on his face. "The dynamics of our relationship at the time weren't as strong as they should have been."

"What about now?"

He lifted a brow. "Now?"

"The dynamics of your relationship now? I couldn't help but notice the time you're spending on her case and with her."

"I'm doing my job. She's in a dangerous situation."

"So you've assigned yourself as her personal bodyguard—"

Patrick didn't wait for her to finish. "I'm a detective and yes, I'm doing my best to keep her safe. Amber is still a friend."

She raised an eyebrow. "A friend? Is that all she is to you?"

Infuriated by the surge of emotion that her question brought, Patrick inhaled a long breath through clenched teeth. "I need to get going. Whoever is after Amber is a loose cannon. We need to get him off the street." Before Liza had the opportunity to agree with him or question him further, he turned and walked out the door.

Twenty minutes later, Patrick pulled up to the front of the battered-women's shelter, parked by the curb and climbed out of his truck, trying his best to dispel Liza's perception, but having a hard time doing so.

He *had* taken on the role of Amber's personal bodyguard.

He had definitely stepped out of his professional scope. It wasn't his place to take on the task to personally protect her.

Even if the tug in his heart told him differently.

Maybe it might be time to back off some. He'd already beefed up patrols in her area.

Then again, nothing seemed to deter her attacker.

Patrick continued at a steady clip down the walk toward the building, his mind at war with his emotions.

He barely got enough rest now. He'd never sleep at night if he had to wonder if Amber was safe.

His emotions winning, he pressed the doorbell. He would do as much for any friend, he told himself.

"Can I help you?" the voice crackled through the intercom on the wall beside the door.

"Detective Patrick Wiley, here to pick up Amber Talbot."

He had a job to do, and his mission objective was to keep Amber safe.

THIRTEEN

After Amber slid into the passenger seat of the SUV, Patrick rounded the front and slipped in behind the wheel.

She dropped her messenger bag on the floor by her feet and buckled her seat belt.

"I've been meaning to ask, what's in that thing?" Patrick's amused look made her smile.

"What? My little tote?"

"Little?" He broke into a full-fledged grin, sending her heart skittering. "I'm surprised you can even pick it up." He started the SUV and pulled away from the curb.

Ah. He underestimated her. She bit the inside of her cheek to hold in a chuckle. She loved it when Patrick relaxed. And that smile. She almost sighed.

Amber blinked, sat more erect. "Actually, it's not too heavy and just big enough for everything I need. My purse, a few files and notes, makeup, a hairbrush, toothbrush, gum and mints, pens, markers, my computer tablet and an umbrella."

He glanced over at her, and she added, "Oh, and a granola bar."

"Is that all?"

"Pretty much."

"I figured something like that. Or a bag of bricks." He

laughed as he pulled onto the thoroughfare and headed down the road toward the community center.

"Feels like it sometimes." She loved this side of Patrick. "So how did your day go?"

"Well, we're piecing things together. Liza dug up some new information that looks promising."

"Liza… She must be good at her job."

"She great. Don't know how I'd get by without her."

Amber swallowed, a sudden thickness in her throat. She glanced out the window. "She's quite lovely," she said after a moment. "You're fortunate to have someone like her in your life."

A stunned silence followed the comment.

She glanced at him just long enough to notice his furrowed brow.

Great. He was probably wondering how to respond. Even more, wondering why she was prying into his personal life and making assumptions—like a nosey ex-girlfriend.

Stupid. Stupid. Stupid. Heat swarmed Amber's body and her pulse kicked up. Chagrin inched in. She drifted down in her seat.

Up ahead the traffic light turned red. Patrick braked and the SUV slowed to a stop. As they waited for the light, Patrick glanced at her. "About Liza—"

"Patrick, I'm sorry." Amber waved off any explanation. "You don't have to explain anything. It's none of my business," she concluded, hoping to put a plug in the conversation.

"Well, thank you. Although, I'm not sure what I have to explain."

Of course he didn't owe her an explanation for anything. She stared out the window, willing the light to turn green.

"I'm just curious. How did you…um, put me and Liza together?"

Great. Apparently he did want to talk about this. "Well…" Anxiety raised her voice to a crackly high pitch. "You were out with her the day you introduced us." Okay, that sounded lame, even to her own ears. Although better than admitting that she had an overactive imagination and the thought of seeing him out with any woman made her stomach knot. Nope, not a confession she wanted him to hear or believe herself.

"Ah, you assumed we were on a date?"

Her heart pounding, she managed a nod.

"You know, it's never safe to assume, because I'm not dating Liza." There was a teasing reprimand in his voice.

Her face got hotter. Her gaze snapped to his. "You're right. Sometimes my imagination gets the best of me." Because that didn't sound any better, she clamped her lips.

The twinkling in his eyes told her he was enjoying watching her squirm. Her heart that was sputtering before was now doing laps in her chest.

Okay, so maybe he wasn't interested in Liza. An arctic chill rippled through her body, giving an unnerving jolt of reality.

It was hard enough to be around him assuming he was involved with someone. But single and unattached, a whole new battle began—between her heart and her head.

Right now her emotions were winning.

She swallowed and forcefully tamped down her feelings. "So what information did Liza supply you with today?"

Patrick flipped the blinker on and turned down the road leading to the community center. "Well, it has to do with a drug ring, offshore trust accounts and Randall and Carl."

As if her mind wasn't already clogged with information, confusion took on a whole new meaning. "I'm not sure where I fit into all this."

"We're still in the speculating mode. I'll bring you up to speed a little later."

Good. Because as of now, her mental capacity was about shot.

Inside the Port City Community Center in downtown Savannah, Amber took Patrick on a tour of the reception hall, where the fund-raiser was slated to take place. It was a huge open room, with a high domed ceiling, glittering chandeliers and gold velvet curtains. The elegant setting was a stark contradiction to the gritty topic of the Silence No More fund-raiser—the prevention of violent crimes against women.

For the next thirty minutes, Patrick stood on the sidelines and waited as Penny Roberts, the community center's event planner, walked Amber through the planned itinerary for the evening. The glint of enthusiasm in Amber's wide green eyes snagged his heart. This was a personal venture for her, and he would do anything to ensure that the fund-raiser would go on as planned.

But deep inside he knew every passing day decreased the likelihood of that happening.

"I believe we've covered everything." Penny Roberts's voice cut through his meandering and redirected his thoughts. She tucked her clipboard under her arm. "Do you have any questions, Ms. Talbot?"

"I can't think of any. Everything sounds perfect." Amber nodded. "Thank you."

"You've put a lot of work into this fund-raiser, and I expect it will a nice evening," Penny said as she turned to leave.

"I can't wait." Amber's lips curved into an appreciative smile. That smile wasn't directed at him, but it touched something inside him. Her loveliness was so evident. Her innocence and humility. His throat tightened. For a moment he forgot the reason he was there.

Memories washed over him. Sweet remembrances of Amber, of their life together. And with each fleeting memory his heart squeezed, bumping up his pulse and weakening his ability to think clearly. He missed Amber. Missed the relationship they'd once had. What he wouldn't give to turn back the clock.

Amber turned slowly to face him. "What do you think, Patrick?"

Patrick ignored the sudden surge in his pulse as Amber's engaging green gaze latched on to his. Suddenly embarrassed by his erratic reflections, he kicked them aside, relieved when rational thoughts that had momentarily deserted him started to form in his brain.

All romantic notions instantly drained from his mind. Losing Amber once had been hard enough. Some things were better off left alone. Like love and relationships.

Widening his stance, he managed a deep breath, then covered his unease with a grin. "What do I think about the fund-raiser?"

Amber shook her head, chuckling. "Yes, does everything sound all right to you?"

Except for the timing. But that was a subject he'd broach again in a few days. "The room is really nice. The itinerary sounds great. I look forward to attending."

Her eyes went wide, and the lethal smile was back. "So if the creep who's after me is behind bars and the fund-raiser goes on as planned, will you still attend?"

Patrick kept his rational thoughts in the forefront of his mind. Still, the playful twinkle in Amber's gaze warmed him deep inside, and he said, "I wouldn't miss it."

Daylight was dying around them as they headed back to his SUV on deck four of the parking garage. Patrick cast an assessing glance around the area, which was half-

full with staff and visitor cars. The few dimly lit fluores-
cent lights flickered overhead. Amber stayed close beside
him. So close he was tempted to slip his arm around her.

Crazy the way his mind worked. Even scary. Inhaling
slowly, he bridled the emotion and shoved his hands into
his pockets.

"So, Patrick, tell me about the drug ring and offshore-
account theory you're working on."

"Well, we now believe both Carl and Randall were involved in the drug trade. If that's true, then we suspect
there's somebody in a higher position who doesn't want
his name out."

Amber's steps stalled. She glanced up, her dark lashes a
feathery surround to the solemn look in her eyes. "So you
think someone besides Carl and Randall wants me dead?"

Patrick stopped, gave a simple shrug. "It's beginning
to look—"

He never finished the sentence. Before he could say
another word, the parking garage exploded in whirr of
gunfire. Three rapid blasts rang out against the aged ce-
ment walls.

Amber shrieked, and instinctively Patrick grabbed her,
whisking her behind a concrete pillar. He pulled his Glock
from his holster. "Get between those two cars," he shouted
to her, gesturing to the row of vehicles to his right. "Stay
down and call 9-1-1."

Amber hurried forward, slipping into the cramped space
between a truck and sedan.

Weapon ready, heart racing, Patrick's gaze swept the
parking deck, taking in any potential threat. No movement. No one in sight. He yelled, "I'm with the Savannah-
Chatham Police Department. Step out with your hands in
the air." His voice echoed around the hollow space like a
boomerang.

No reply came. Patrick stared down at the long row of

cars. Whoever was out there had to be behind one of the vehicles or inside one.

He slowly moved forward, watching for any movement, listening. Tightening his grip on his gun, he leveled it solidly in front of him.

A hush settled in the air, spine-chilling, deafening. His adrenaline was skyrocketing. It was time to take this guy down.

A deep grunt broke the silence, then the echo of footsteps.

Patrick searched frantically for the shooter. He caught a flicker of movement in the shadows. The hint of a person edging toward the north exit of the parking deck. "Step out and put your hands in the air!" Patrick barked the order for a second and final time.

Another crack of gunfire rent the air.

Patrick spun and took refuge behind a parked car. He swiveled in a crouch and fired back.

The air settled. Silence crept in again.

Patrick took several deep breaths, waiting and listening for the man to make another move. Twenty seconds was long enough. He peeked around the car bumper, saw nothing, ducked back. Then he turned, casting a quick look toward the area where Amber was hidden. He couldn't see her, but prayed she was still huddled low and safe.

The scent of lingering gunpowder assaulted his nose. His nostrils flared and he got moving again. Heart hammering, he kept his back plastered to the concrete wall and positioned himself to watch the exit door and keep Amber's location in his periphery.

Another sharp pop ripped through the air, and Patrick pulled back as a bullet whizzed past him, burying itself into the wall an inch from his head.

Dropping low, he gritted his teeth. That was too close. Long shadows fell across the parking deck. Patrick surveyed the area, mopping sweat from his brow with his sleeve. Eighty feet away, on the far side of the deck, the ominous figure made his way toward the elevator. But Patrick would not let his assailant get away.

As if reading Patrick's mind, the figure stopped and fired again, the blast ricocheting around the space.

In response, Patrick aimed through the opening of two concrete barriers and squeezed off two rounds.

He heard a shriek, followed by a loud grunt of pain.

Got him. "Okay, creep. It's time to give up!"

A feral growl, then the tall, burly man, waving two pistols, one in each hand, came stumbling down through the row of cars, screaming, "I'm not finished with you yet!" His eyes were wide and crazed. His face was bloodied, but only from what looked to be a superficial head wound. The bullet had only grazed him.

"Where is she?" The man picked up speed and was aiming his weapon in Amber's direction.

Patrick jumped to his feet. "Amber, stay put!"

Another round of gunfire rang out.

Patrick had no choice. He aimed his Glock and pulled the trigger. Nothing.

What? Heart ready to explode, Patrick made a decision. He took off in a run toward the madman that was shooting in Amber's direction. "Freeze! Police."

Amber's frantic scream echoed around him as the man shifted his aim and fired at Patrick.

The bullet caught him in the shoulder. The force flung him against a car, and blood spewed from his ripped muscle, spreading rapidly across his shirt.

"No! No! Patrick!" That was from Amber.

A lancing pain splintered through Patrick's shoulder, and he gritted his teeth. Pushing past the sting, he lunged toward the man, taking him down in one clumsy swoop.

The guns flew out of the thug's hands and went spinning across the concrete floor.

Patrick drove his knee into the man's spine and locked his uninjured arm around his adversary's thick neck. "Who are you?" Patrick spat out, praying the blood pouring from his shoulder wouldn't cause him to pass out before backup got there.

"Get off me, man!" The thug writhed against Patrick's hold.

Patrick held him in place, digging his knee deeper into the man's back. "I'm going to ask you one more time. Who are you?"

Still the man continued to wrestle.

"He asked who you were."

Patrick looked up to find Amber holding one of the man's guns. Her grip was shaky, but she kept the weapon trained on the goon.

"Go on. Tell him who you are. And why are you trying to kill me?" He detected some heat in her voice now.

Patrick was so proud of her, he could almost smile.

"Okay. Okay. I'm…Darrell. Darrell Ott," the man grunted out.

Still holding him down, Patrick leaned in closer, just an inch from his ear. "Darrell, the nice lady here asked why you were shooting at her."

Darrell squirmed and Patrick clamped down harder. "Okay, man! I got a call a couple hours ago. Got instructions. Time. Location. The target's name. You know the drill."

"Who called you?" Amber took over.

"The General," he spat out. "I work for the General."

Patrick's interest piqued. "Who is the General?"

Sirens blared, loud and approaching. Finally.

Light-headed, with his head pounding, Patrick steadied his grip on Darrell, his limbs getting weaker by the moment. He was in trouble. He swallowed, his mouth suddenly dry. "Darrell," he growled, using every bit of energy he could muster. "The General. Who is he?"

"I don't know, man. He calls himself the General, that's all I know."

"Patrick, you don't look good. Are you all right?" Amber's panicked voice echoed in his ears.

Patrick glanced down. Blood continued to gush down his shirt and onto his pants. Pressure built against his lungs as he fought for a full breath. "Just keep holding the gun, sweetheart. You're doing great."

A mob of police officers burst onto the deck through every exit door.

"Get an ambulance!" Amber called out. "Now!"

That was the last thing Patrick heard before he crumpled onto the concrete, striking the floor with an echoing thud.

FOURTEEN

Amber disliked hospital rooms even more than she loathed cold, lonely ER cubicles, or being transported in EMS vehicles. Although she did her best to avoid each, during the past sixteen hours she'd been unfortunate enough to experience all three.

Only this time, she hadn't been the patient. Instead, she was the unscathed target the maniac shooter had missed, all because Patrick had taken the bullet in her place.

At St. Joseph's Hospital in downtown Savannah, Amber sat quietly in the corner of Patrick's room, curled up in one of those uncomfortable oversize hospital chairs, watching him sleep. Her heart crimped at the sight of Patrick in the hospital bed, with bandages covering his shoulder and his arm in a sling, because of her.

She took a deep breath, wiped a tear from her eye. Patrick had put his life in danger to save hers.

The only thing keeping her from a complete meltdown was the knowledge that he hadn't been killed.

She'd stayed with him in the ambulance, and then in the ER, where he was stabilized before being taken to surgery. More than two hours had dragged by as she and Vance had sat and waited to hear from the surgeon. Every passing second had heightened the sadness and growing concern.

She'd tried to relax, even managed to pray, but the waiting had been brutal. Finally after three hours the doctor had walked in, dressed in green scrubs with a surgical mask dangling from his neck.

Both she and Vance had been out of their seats and halfway across the waiting room before the doctor had a chance to look for them. Swiftly and succinctly the doc had gone over Patrick's condition, detailing the challenges of the meticulous surgery. The bullet had fractured Patrick's scapula, and barely missed his subclavian artery, a major vessel that if nicked could have caused him to bleed to death.

Patrick had lost plenty of blood, but after three units of packed red blood cells and multiple bags of saline, the doctor had given him a positive prognosis. Something she would be eternally grateful for.

Now Amber shifted uncomfortably against the vinyl cushion. She felt exhausted and drained, but the numbness that had possessed her since the shooting was finally wearing off. A menacing ache filled its place as she pondered the events of the past sixteen hours.

It had been a whirlwind. Everything had happened so fast. From the gunfire, to the crazed man coming at her with a gun, to Patrick getting shot.

Patrick had gotten shot.

Amber rubbed her hands over her face. She still couldn't believe it.

Tears stung the back of her eyes for the umpteenth time since Vance had left her a couple of hours ago to head home to get some sleep. She blinked them back.

Sleep wasn't on her agenda for the foreseeable future. She wondered if she could ever really rest again knowing what she'd put Patrick through.

With her heart sinking fast in her chest, she summoned up the protective numbness that she'd relied on over the years. Facing reality had never been easy.

But never had reality hurt like this.

A gentle snore broke through the hush in the room.

Shaken out of her funk, Amber got to her feet and padded softly to Patrick's bed. She adjusted his blankets, mindful not to disturb the pillows supporting his shoulder or the blue sling and swathe immobilizing his arm. Bracing herself against a rush of emotions, she thanked God that he was safe. A soft glow breathed down from the small light on the wall. Shadows faintly danced over Patrick's features. He looked relaxed and peaceful, thanks to the pain medication. Which hopefully wouldn't wear off for hours.

Until then, she'd continue to watch him. Kissing the tips of two fingers, she brushed them along his cheek. She hoped he could forgive her.

She made her way back to the corner of the room and melted back in the chair. She unfolded the blanket the nurse had supplied her with and wrapped it tightly around her. Night was always the worst, but no other night compared to this one.

Time crawled by, until finally early-morning sunlight filtered in through the window. She closed her eyes, feeling a sudden warmth on her face, an odd contradiction to the pervasive chill that had settled deep in her bones.

She had managed to do the one thing she never wanted to do again—hurt Patrick Wiley. She'd made one complicated mistake that continued to snowball, and here she was, eleven years later, still hurting him. And he had a bullet-size hole in his shoulder as a remembrance of her.

A tear leaked down her cheek and she brushed it away. As much as she cared for Patrick, even loved him, he was much better off without her around.

Last evening's incident had proved that fact.

Heaving a sigh, she chastised herself for being impulsive. After all this time, she hadn't learned. She'd been so wrapped up in trying to keep her fund-raiser on track, she'd never stopped to consider that by Patrick's commitment to keep her safe, she'd put him in danger, too.

Why had she been so selfish? Why hadn't she listened and postponed the fund-raiser? Why hadn't she jumped at the chance of going to a safe house, instead of marching into the community center? Why hadn't she trusted her gut eleven years ago and said no to the party?

Why? Why? Why? She slouched back in her chair, rubbing her face. Stubborn. Impulsive. *Lord, forgive me.*

A trickle of peace seeped through her.

God did care.

And more than anything she wanted Him to walk with her through this. Be with her forever.

She'd spent too many years living in denial, enveloped in a dark cloud of guilt and sadness. Alone and afraid to trust, love or even believe.

A place she didn't want to be anymore.

"Good morning."

At Patrick's soft greeting, Amber looked up. Suddenly the morning seemed brighter. "Good morning, Patrick."

She pushed up from the chair and walked to him, almost dizzy with relief when she caught his wan smile. But her relief was short-lived, cut short by the painful grimace tightening his face as he shifted in bed. "Patrick, shall I call the nurse?"

"No, I just moved too quickly." Patrick's voice stayed low but strong as he carefully repositioned his shoulder against his pillows. "Okay, that's better."

Blinking hard to hold back tears, she said a simple prayer. *Lord, be with Patrick.* She swallowed. "Are you in a lot of pain?"

"I'm pretty sore. But even worse than the pain is my frustration and anger about what went down last night. And, I also hate the idea of being cooped up in this hospital."

She felt the same way, minus the pain. That was unless she counted the ache in her heart. "Patrick, I'm so sorry about last night…" The rest of her apology stuck in her throat. She couldn't truly express how badly she felt.

"You're sorry?" he asked. "I'm the one who should be sorry. No spare weapon? That Glock carried me through the war. It was always dependable. Until today. I'll know better next time."

Before she could respond to that, Patrick latched on to the metal side rail and tried to pull himself up. An inch or two from the mattress, he clenched his teeth, crumbling back against the sheets with a groan.

"Let me help you." Amber pressed the button to raise the head of the bed.

Loosening his grip on the railing, Patrick blew out a breath. "Thank you. Maybe you should call the nurse."

Amber pressed the call bell and, as they waited for the nurse to bring some medication, she adjusted Patrick's blankets. "It's just horrible what happened." She stuffed another pillow behind his head.

He cut her off from saying more with a shake of his head. "Amber, I don't blame you for me getting shot. In fact, you saved my life. So thank you."

He was thanking her? The poor man was delirious. "Patrick, I didn't save your life. I put you in danger. You gave me good advice and I didn't listen. Not since this case started. Not eleven years ago. And because of that you were almost killed."

"That's a bit of a stretch." He winced as he shifted slightly. "So what you're telling me is since you didn't take my advice, that makes the man that shot me not guilty."

"Yes… I mean no." She rubbed a hand across her forehead. "You obviously don't understand what I'm trying to say."

"What I do understand is that you're not responsible for the actions of others."

For a moment Amber let those words circulate in her thoughts. The pause that followed was intense, filled with Patrick's unwavering gaze. She had to admit he was right.

She managed to nod.

"I have some more advice for you, and I want you to take it very seriously."

Bracing herself, she held her breath as Patrick lifted his good arm and reached up to run his thumb down her cheek. His gaze warm on hers, he said, "Stop feeling guilty and let go of the past."

It was very good advice…something she was working on. "But—"

"No buts," he said, a little too authoritatively, still cradling her cheek.

She finally managed a weak "Okay," too frazzled to argue. At the moment, breathing was enough of a challenge.

"We still have a case to solve. A killer is still on the loose and possibly an accomplice. And we need to get you set up in a safe house."

She nodded her assent. Considering Patrick's injury, Amber was surprised by his resolve to continue on the case. Apparently, he took his police oath seriously. No, she amended, honor and integrity were what drove him.

Once again she couldn't help be impressed with this man.

A few hours later, Patrick sat in bed, propped up with pillows and caught in a midmorning funk. He had a million things he should be doing, and here he was laid up in the hospital for the next… He sucked in through his teeth, hating to even guess.

Outside of his incredibly sore shoulder, he wasn't feel-

ing too bad, except he was starving. And this hospital food
was a far cry from…well, food.

Patrick picked at the powdered scrambled eggs on his
tray. Way too salty. His failed attempt to spice them up
backfired. Now they were barely edible. He took a bite of
grits, and almost gagged. Something about lumpy grits.

A swig of coffee helped wash it down. He laid down
his fork. "How's your breakfast?" He directed his question to Amber, whose hospital-issued breakfast tray sat on
a small rolling table beside her, roughly untouched. Not
that he blamed her.

She glanced up at him, her eyes weary. Dark circles bore
witness to her sleepless night. She looked exhausted. "It's
fine. I'm not that hungry."

"You need to eat something."

"You're right." She nodded, the shadows beneath her
eyes deepening. She picked up a plastic fork.

Patrick barely shifted, attempting to reposition his arm,
and winced. He was gaining a whole new respect for bullets.

"Are you all right?"

"I'd be better without this sling thing." He tugged with
his free hand on the fabric. "It's uncomfortable and awkward. I'm not even sure how it's helping."

"It's there to support your shoulder." Amber set down
her fork and instantly she was at his side. She adjusted
the Velcro strap on the sling, allowing a little more give.
"It that better?"

"Yes. Very." Somehow having Amber dote on him
seemed to make everything better. It was not something
he needed to get used to, but for now he'd enjoy it.

"By the way, I sent Vance a text and asked him to arrange for an officer to come by to take you to the safe
house."

"The safe house? Today?" Amber parted her lips to say more, but he shot her a warning look.

"You're exhausted and you can rest there. Right now it's the safest place for you."

She nodded. "Okay."

He hadn't expected such a compliant response so quickly. He thought at least she'd argue to stay and take care of him. Not that he'd reconsider that.

Still, his ego deflated some.

"I'll have the officer drop by Kim's house and let you pick up a few things."

She nodded again.

The door opened and Vance appeared with a brown paper grocery bag in one hand and a white take-out sack from Gus's in the other. "Here are the clothes that you asked for, and I thought you might like this." He dropped the white sack next to Patrick's breakfast tray on the rolling bedside table.

"Vance, you're a lifesaver." Patrick unwrapped a biscuit and offered Amber a piece.

"No, thanks." She held up a hand.

"Where do you want these clothes?" Vance held up the paper bag.

"Over there is fine." Patrick gestured with his biscuit to the corner of the room.

"Clothes?" Amber said. "Won't you be in the hospital for another couple days?"

"That's the plan." Patrick swallowed his food.

"Actually, I'm making it an order." Vance hiked up a thick brow. "I talked to the doctor and asked him not to discharge you until you were one hundred percent ready. Although I must say you look more rested than I feel." He smirked, then said to Amber, "You look pretty tired, too."

"I am," she said softly.

"Painkillers make for a restful and sound sleep," Patrick said. Actually, a little too sound. He'd fallen asleep to the gentle sound of Amber talking to him, and the next thing he knew three hours had passed.

"How is your pain?" Vance sprawled into a nearby chair, yawning.

"Good." Patrick lifted his arm as a show of good faith. Then immediately regretted it when a surge of pain shot through his shoulder like a knife. "That is," he corrected through clenched teeth, "as long as I don't move my arm or my shoulder."

Vance's phone rang.

"That's what I figured. So take it easy." Vance's deep-set eyes narrowed, then he stood up and slipped out of the room to answer the call.

"Let me help you." Amber went about adjusting his pillows again. "Remember, you don't want to overdo it. If you don't take the time to heal, you'll be right back in here and my case will never get solved."

She had good advice.

And a gentle touch.

He liked that. Probably too much.

"That's good news." Vance's voice could be heard from the hall. "I'll be right there." He burst back through the doorway of Patrick's room.

Both Patrick and Amber's attention turned to Vance.

"Darrell Ott has been squawking like a windbag fili-busterer since he got there. Finally he gave us something we could use. And wouldn't you know, good ole Randall Becker's name came up. The officer tailing Randall just arrested him. He's being hauled into the station now."

"Kicking and screaming, I'm sure." Patrick would have loved to be there to greet the man. "Did Ott say Randall referred to himself as the General?"

Vance gave a quick shake of his head. "He's holding fast to his claim that he doesn't know who the General is."

"Keep pushing him," Patrick said.

"You know I will." On that note, Vance headed toward the door, then stopped short and glanced back at Patrick. "Get some rest, Wiley. Don't worry, we've got this one."

Patrick smiled. He had full confidence in Vance. But rest and not worry? Easier said than done.

FIFTEEN

As Amber finished washing up in Patrick's hospital room bathroom, she cupped her hands and splashed cold water on her face, hoping to rejuvenate her sagging spirit.

She shivered against the chill, but instead of feeling refreshed, despair hung in her heart, achy and heavy.

Grabbing a handful of paper towels, she blotted the moisture from her face.

Just moments ago she'd been keyed up with optimism knowing that Randall Becker had been picked up and was being brought in for questioning. Clues were coming together. The case was progressing and hopefully coming to a close. But now, as she readied to leave for the safe house, she felt an all-too-familiar tug in her chest. A reminder that once her assailant was caught, she would slip back into her old life.

And Patrick would slip back into his.

Considering all the grief she'd caused Patrick, he should be thankful—and she should be relieved. She never wanted an opportunity to hurt him again.

A logical statement. But her emotions continued to play tug-of-war in her chest. She told herself to be glad she was leaving for the safe house. She needed some time alone to process the myriad emotions writhing through her.

Fairy-tale endings never came true, she reminded herself.

Sighing, she crumpled up the paper towels and threw them into the trash. She found her thoughts returning to Patrick's earlier statement. *Stop feeling guilty and let go of the past.*

In short—move on.

More than anything she wanted to do that. But one look at Patrick and that theory was blown to pieces.

She needed to accept what her heart already knew: Patrick would never be the man for her. There was too much history. Too much time apart.

Amber breathed deeply, and as she grabbed her bag to leave, the mirror above the sink caught her reflection. She grimaced at the pallid image staring back at her. She leaned closer. Was it the lighting or did she always looked this washed out?

Fighting another sigh, Amber pinched her cheeks to rouse some color and moistened her lips with her tongue. Then after combing her fingers through her tangle of curls, she took a step back. Rechecking her appearance, she arched an eyebrow at her reflection. Now she looked washed out and disheveled.

Plunging her hand into her purse, she fished out a few clips. Then, lifting her hair, she twisted it into a loose bun and gave another assessing glance in the mirror.

Not great, but better. Although, she reminded herself, she had no one to impress. She snatched up her bag and flung it onto her shoulder.

She walked out of the bathroom to find Patrick asleep. His breathing, soft and rhythmic, filled the tight space. She tiptoed past his bed and sank into the same chair that had been her bed for the night. Uncomfortable then. Uncomfortable now.

She shifted softly, eyeing her watch, wondering what

time the officer would arrive to whisk her off to safe housing. Her heart pinched in her chest. She wanted nothing more than to stay with Patrick. For once, to be the one to watch over him.

But that wasn't going to happen. And she needed to accept that.

Closing her eyes, she lifted a prayer. *Father, I want to trust You. Please guide my thoughts and show me the path You want me on and help me to stay on it.*

A gentle warmth draped her heart and cocooned her soul.

She knew from experience how much easier it was to stray than to follow. But for the first time in forever, she was willing to fully put her trust in the Lord.

As she opened her eyes, Tony emerged from the hospital hallway. "Morning, kiddo," he said in a whisper.

Amber got to her feet and pressed a finger to her lips.

He nodded in understanding.

She padded softly toward him.

Are you okay? Tony mouthed, his gaze stormy, his rigid body language exhibiting unease.

She nodded.

"Let's talk." He gestured toward the door. "Would you like to go to the cafeteria and grab something to eat?"

"I can't." She kept her voice low and glanced toward Patrick's bed and him sleeping in it. "An officer will be here any minute. He'll be taking me to a safe house."

"A safe house?" Tony whispered back.

Amber nodded. "I'll be there hopefully only a few days."

"Good. Things are getting pretty dangerous for you out here."

Amber's breathing accelerated as she thought about the dangerous situations she'd already been in. A little seclusion was sounding better all the time. "Patrick and the other detectives feel as though they're close to a break in the case."

Tony grinned, pulling her into a quick embrace. "That's good news. Exactly what we're all hoping for. This nightmare to soon be over."

"Excuse me." The nurse, whose name badge read Jane, entered, letting the door swing closed behind her. With a syringe in her hand, she walked up to Patrick and started to raise the head of his bed. "Mr. Wiley, I have some medication for you."

For a split second, Patrick jolted upright, before collapsing back against the pillow, his complexion chalky. "Ow!"

The urge to run to Patrick's side and comfort him overwhelmed Amber, and she had to stop herself. It was the nurse's job, not hers.

"Sorry to startle you, Mr. Wiley," the nurse said, pulling an alcohol wipe from her scrub pocket. "But I have some pain medication for you."

Patrick's answer came quick. "No, just bring me some ibuprofen, please."

The nurse tore open the package. "Ibuprofen won't be enough to keep your pain under control."

The nurse's statement sounded logical, but Patrick didn't appear to even consider it.

"My pain is under control. I just need some ibuprofen." The tight grimace on his face completely refuted his claim.

"Patrick, it might be a good idea to take the medication." Amber jumped in and tried to reinforce the nurse's advice. "It will help you rest."

Patrick shook his head, his color slowly returning. "The last narcotic they gave me hit me like a tranquilizer dart."

"That's why the doctor ordered it." The nurse was curt. "To help you rest, as well as control your pain."

Patrick didn't miss a beat. "I believe as a patient I have the right to refuse any medication that's ordered."

Nurse Jane exchanged a look with Amber.

Amber gave a half shrug. "He's pretty hard to convince."

"Okay. The doctor will be in shortly. He can discuss pain-management options with Mr. Wiley." The nurse directed her comment to Amber as she made for the door, obviously inferring that Amber had some influence over Patrick—like maybe a wife or a girlfriend. A very wrong assumption. "In the meantime, I'll get an order for ibuprofen. There's a call bell, if he changes his mind."

"All right." Amber nodded.

"I sure hate what happened last night, Patrick." Tony's voice made her refocus. She twisted around as Tony approached Patrick's bed. "I had second thoughts about Amber going to the appointment at the community center. I wish I had offered to go myself."

Grief struck Amber, as did the reminder that she should have canceled the appointment altogether. "Tony, you're not responsible at all. Both you and Patrick asked me to postpone the fund-raiser. I should have listened."

Tony and Patrick stared at her.

"I thought I was doing the right thing—the brave thing," she went on, feeling the need to explain. Not that her admission would change anything. But hopefully her motivation made sense, not only to them, but also to herself. "This guy pushed me into a tailspin once eleven years ago, and I never wanted to give him that leverage again."

Patrick listened as Amber poured out her heart, wishing there was something he could do to ease her pain. Every time she reiterated her guilt, it just hammered home how violated she'd felt by what happened to her.

After eleven years she was still trying to make amends. Her redemption? To help others like herself. She was the bravest woman he knew.

And beautiful, both inside and out. Now with her hair swept up in a messy bun, he could barely think straight.

Before Patrick realized what was happening, Tony sidled up to Amber and slipped his arm around her shoulder. As he whispered something to her, she responded by leaning in closer. For a long moment they stood there together, quiet and serene.

Patrick's heart rattled against his ribs—he was not at all comfortable with what he was seeing. A week ago he might have not been this unnerved, telling himself he was glad Tony was there for her. But after being around her the past few days...nothing was that black-and-white anymore.

Several heartbeats passed, and Patrick breathed relief when Amber shifted away from Tony. She drew herself up tall, as if gaining composure.

"Amber, I'll be looking in on Patrick while you're away. I'm sure he'll keep me abreast on everything that's happening."

Amber nodded at Tony. "Hopefully I'll see you in a few days."

Patrick's phone rang, and Amber reached for it before he had the chance. She handed it to him.

"Thank you." He smiled, and was pleased when she reciprocated.

Officer Blake Carson was on the line. Patrick listened as Carson fed him a long-winded explanation of why he was running late to pick up Amber. Getting the gist of it, Patrick halted the conversation. "Just finish up with whatever you have to do. I hope to see you soon."

"It shouldn't be too long, sir."

"Thanks." Patrick clicked off the receiver.

"Is everything okay?"

Patrick met Amber's concerned gaze. "Nothing critical." Patrick tucked his phone in the pocket of his hospital gown. "The officer who will be taking you to the safe house arrived about thirty minutes ago and somehow got pulled into a security issue with one of the patient's family members here at the hospital. After he finishes up some paperwork, he'll be right up to get you."

"Actually, I'm about to leave," Tony said. "I wouldn't mind walking with Amber to the security office."

Patrick started to say he'd rather Amber wait for the officer, then he remembered the doctor would be in to speak with him soon. And he had a few questions he preferred to discuss with him in private—mainly how soon he could get out of there. "Tony, that would be great."

He glanced back at Amber. "I'll let security know you're on your way. And leave your cell phone on until you get to the safe house."

"All right." Amber started gathering her things, and then halted. "I don't have my cell phone. I must have left it in the bathroom."

As Amber took off for the bathroom, Tony hoisted up her messenger bag.

"This thing feels like a ton of bricks."

"I believe it's her survival kit." Patrick's attempt to laugh came out like a groan. He blew out a breath and repositioned his shoulder.

Patrick's phone rang again. This time it was Vance. As Patrick listened to the latest update, Amber passed quietly out the door with Tony with only a slight wave. He'd hoped to have a final word with her. Remind her to stay safe and not worry.

Maybe even hug her goodbye.

Where had that come from? He'd crossed enough lines already.

Gripping the receiver, Patrick kicked that idea aside and pushed his thoughts into investigator mode.

SIXTEEN

Amber hiked the strap of her bag higher on her shoulder and slipped into the elevator behind Tony. The hospital patient transporter who shared the tight space maneuvered his oversize wheelchair to the left, offering them a little more room. Amber leaned against the wall and fought off a yawn. Tony pressed the necessary button and they started to descend.

A wave of nausea rolled through her. She pressed a hand on her abdomen and drew in a steadying breath. She was exhausted, and desperate for the truth and for her perpetrator to be caught.

The elevator bounced to a stop and the doors slid open with a hollow ding. The man in blue scrubs nodded. "Go ahead. This isn't my floor."

Amber pressed by the man and followed Tony out and down a long hallway, a blank slate of stark white walls, closed doors and dark speckled floors.

"It's this way," Tony assured her, as if he could read her mind.

A hushed, almost cave-like silence permeated the corridor. Not a single employee or patient was anywhere to be seen. She directed her curiosity to the area around her, searching for the security office, wondering if they'd gotten off on the wrong floor.

They stepped through a set of sliding doors and beyond

the threshold where the hallway came to an end. A red exit sign beamed above a single door to the left.

The sliding door slowly coasted shut behind them, and Tony paused. "Oh, I just remembered that you'd stepped out of the room when security called Patrick back. There was another delay, and Patrick asked if I could drop you by Kim's house. Another officer will meet us there. He suggested we use this back exit so you leaving would be less conspicuous."

It took Amber a moment to process that. "But Patrick didn't want me to leave without an officer present."

Tony gave an offhanded shrug. "I'm not sure what all transpired. But I do know he wants you at the safe house as soon as possible."

Second thoughts raced around in her head, weakening her resolve to comply with Patrick's wishes for her to leave for the safe house right then. It didn't make sense for her not to wait until someone could pick her up there. The hospital was secure.

As if reading her mind Tony added, "I think it's hard for Patrick to rest when he's worried about you."

Reality blasted any thread of rationale she could muster about why she should stay. Patrick didn't need her there; he was well taken care of. And with her gone, maybe he'd take some of those pain meds. "You're right, Tony. Patrick does need his rest."

And she had no plan to rob him of that.

"Ready?" Tony pushed open the door, holding it for her to go ahead of him. "I don't want to keep the officer waiting."

Amber swallowed and walked out the door, anxiety building like gathering storm clouds. She had no idea what she'd be in for next.

But the moment Amber sank into the plush leather seat in Tony's dual-cab truck, the tension knotting her back and shoulders started to ease. Maybe it was time for a little hiatus, to distance herself from the threats against her, from Patrick.

"Relax and try to rest some before we get to Kim's house." Tony's soft words paralleled her own thoughts.

"Thank you." Settling deeper against the buttery leather, Amber crossed her arms and allowed her eyes to drift shut. The drive wouldn't be long, but a few minutes of rest sounded wonderful.

Patrick sat in his hospital bed, mulling over the data and clues for the case and making an outline for himself, trying to pull the pieces together. From what his gut told him, Carl and Randall had close drug ties, and the General was the local kingpin they answered to.

The narcotics investigative unit was on it, looking into the local drug rings, trying to find a link to Randall or Carl. It was a tight-knit world of drug lords, mules and dealers, dirty money and greed. And they liked to stay under the radar. Incriminating facts were hard to come by and proving them was even harder.

And Randall knew that.

Vance's report that a belligerent Randall had arrived at the station and had stayed uncooperative didn't surprise Patrick. He had no doubt Randall would fight to the bitter end, declaring his innocence without emotion or insight. And so far, he was doing a pretty good job of it.

Nonetheless, Vance's interrogation methods were top-notch, and if anyone could get something out of Randall, Vance could. That fact made being holed up in a hospital and out of commission more tolerable for Patrick.

Although, not much.

Leaning back, Patrick rested against his pillow, ignoring the pulsating pain in his shoulder. He found himself wondering where Darrell Ott fit into all of this. He was curious to see the ballistics results being run on the bullets fired yesterday and match them against those fired at the counseling center.

Ott blatantly denied killing Carl, or making any other attempts on Amber's life.

In Patrick's gut he believed him. Which meant Amber's assailant had hired Ott, a lowlife assassin, to finally get the job done that he couldn't do himself.

This was personal for whoever was after Amber. Someone who knew her.

Maybe someone who hadn't even popped into the picture yet?

A disturbing scenario.

He buried that thought for the moment.

Patrick shifted again and pressed a hand against his thick shoulder dressing, cringing against another spasm of pain. It lasted only a few long seconds, though it was brutal.

He blew out a long breath and pressed the call bell. Maybe he did need something stronger than ibuprofen. At the same time his cell phone buzzed. At first his heart kicked with hope when he saw it was Vance calling, and then skepticism settled in. Vance couldn't be finished talking to Randall already.

Patrick clicked on the phone, pressed it to his ear, hoping against hope for good news. A fact. A clue. A new lead. Something.

"What do you got, Vance?"

"Besides a headache?"

Patrick nodded. "Ditto on that."

"Randall Becker is a tough nut to crack," Vance huffed out.

"But?" Vance had something or he wouldn't have called.

"Well, I painted Becker a pretty grim picture of what

his future held if he intentionally withheld information from the police, and the creep clammed up even tighter."

"I was hoping for good news."

"Well, at least Ott's in custody. We're following up on a few of his leads."

"What about the General? Did Ott own up to knowing any more about him?"

"Still denies knowing anything."

"Do we have enough from Ott to keep Randall behind bars for a few days?"

Vance hesitated, so long, in fact, that Patrick finally said, "Randall's out, isn't he?"

"There was nothing conclusive to hold him on. Hearsay from a hired gun doesn't go far. I had hoped Randall might slip up, tell us something."

Randall was smarter than that. That was what scared Patrick. "Let's keep a tail on him."

A deep chuckle. "You know I will."

"Thanks, Vance." Patrick hung up the phone and dialed Amber's number, grateful she'd agreed to go to the safe house. Hopefully, she was on her way by now.

On the sixth ring, his call went to voice mail. "This is Amber Talbot. I can't pick up right now. Please leave your name and—"

Patrick hung up the phone. Maybe she was already there? He punched Redial for the officer assigned to take her.

"This is Officer Blake Carson."

"Officer Carson, this is Investigator Wiley. Could you put Amber on the line?"

"Amber?"

Patrick straightened in bed so abruptly he jarred his wounded shoulder. He bit his lip against the pain and sharpened his tone. "Yes, Amber Talbot. The woman whom I hope you're in the process of escorting to the safe house."

"Sir, I'm not with Miss Talbot yet. I just finished here and was about to come up there to get her."

"What?" Patrick glanced at the time. "She left here almost an hour ago to meet you in the security office. I called down there and spoke to you, letting you know to expect her."

"Yes, sir, you did. However, she never showed up."

"What do you mean, she never showed up?" Patrick barked into the phone, frustration egging him on, fear twisting his gut. "Run plates on a Tony Hill. See if his vehicle is still in the parking garage. And call a code yellow. Get this hospital on lockdown!"

As Patrick jumped out of bed, he banged his shoulder on the bed railing. Pain blasted through his extremities and stars flashed in his eyes. As his legs nearly buckled, he gripped the edge of the bedside table, bracing himself against the crippling pain.

"Can I help you?" The nurse's voice crackled through the call bell.

Gritting his teeth, Patrick didn't answer. He fought to focus. He needed to get out of there, needed to find Amber.

Exhaling a pent-up breath, he crossed the floor and grabbed the bag Vance had left him. He had no idea what was going down, but he didn't plan to sit around and wait to find out.

He punched Amber's number again. Wedging the phone between his shoulder and jaw, he ripped the brown paper bag open and pulled out his clothes.

No answer still.

Swallowing a groan, he worked past the pain and pulled on his clothes.

His greatest mission was about to begin.

SEVENTEEN

Amber woke to the sound of a cell phone ringing. She blinked her eyes, realizing she'd fallen asleep. For how long, she had no idea. Reaching down, she fumbled around her feet, searching for her bag, surprised when it wasn't there.

The ringing continued, a shrill bleat rising from the backseat. She adjusted her seat belt and reached over the bench seat in search of her phone, but froze as Tony's strong hand clamped onto her wrist.

"You don't need to answer that," Tony said.

Amber's breath hiccupped. "What?"

"I should have turned that off." His burly fingers tightened farther, cutting off the blood flow and making her pulse sprint. "There's no one you need to talk to now. Just relax." His gaze, as sharp as his tone, homed in on her face.

The ringing stopped.

Amber tugged her hand free of his grip and plunked back in her seat, rubbing her sore wrist. Stunned by what had just taken place, she felt dread skip up her spine. In all the years she'd known Tony, she'd never seen him act this way. She lifted her chin and intensified her glare on him. "Tony, what's going on?"

Time ticked by, long anxious moments. Tony's gaze didn't waver and he stayed mute, his eyes fixed on the road in front of them.

An internal bell went off, and Amber darted her gaze out the front windshield. On the side of the road was a sign for North Coastal Highway 25. Her level of panic ratcheted another notch. Why were they heading into the Savannah National Wildlife Refuge and in the opposite direction of Kim's house?

"Tony." Even in her attempt to stay calm, her voice pitched to a near screech. "Where are we going?"

"My dear Amber. You ask too many questions."

Her pulse shot to the red zone. What was going on? The jolt of adrenaline suddenly brought her to full awareness.

Tony was the one who wanted her dead.

But how did he fit in with Carl and Randall? Her mind erupted in confusion. Nothing made sense. Her heart in her throat, she held her composure and ordered herself to stay calm. Maybe she was wrong. There had to be a simple explanation.

Swallowing, she studied Tony: the menacing twist to his features, the grimace on his lips. Amber's chest filled with fear, wondering how someone who had always exhibited such a calm and caring spirit could hide such evil.

She blinked, hoping this was all a bad dream. But when she looked again at the scowl on his face, her body went numb. This was not a dream, but her worst nightmare.

"Tony…you're the one? The one who's been trying—" Disbelief choked off the rest of her words.

A beat passed, then Tony sighed. "Things have gotten very complicated, Amber."

Complicated? What was so complicated that he needed her dead?

A new kind of fear mushroomed in her chest. Moving vehicle or not, she needed to get out of there. Concentrating on escape, Amber unclipped her seat belt and grabbed on to the door handle. She yanked and yanked, meeting resistance. She was locked in.

"Sorry, kiddo. It's locked from the inside. A little mechanism I installed myself." Tony sighed again and shook his head.

Amber's jaw went slack. She firmed it up. "Why are you doing this?"

Tony exhaled a coarse breath. "You've come a long way, my friend, growing to be such a confident and passionate woman. An applaudable accomplishment in many respects, however, vulnerable and broken suited you better."

What? Before Amber could even gasp at his skewed logic, Tony jerked the vehicle to the left, around a sharp bend that led down a narrow gravel service road. The force sent her hurtling into the dash, her palms taking the brunt, sending a spike of pain exploding up her arms and into her back. She fell back against the seat, unconcerned with the pain as her mind stumbled to catch up.

So the fact that she was getting strong posed a threat, even more so now that she'd decided to tell her story. How would that involve Tony? In a flash of clarity she understood. Carl and Randall were dealing drugs. Tony had to be the General.

A shudder ripped down Amber's spine. She stared right at Tony. "I can't believe this. You're a substance abuse counselor and running a drug ring?"

His laugh was hollow and mirthless. "Nothing in life is quite what it seems."

Amber swallowed back bile, knowing his plans for her, but no way was she going to let him succeed.

"Let me out of here!" she snapped. "Do you hear me? Let me go!" Amber yanked on his arm, and the truck started to weave.

Overcorrecting the wheel, Tony roared, "No, you let go of me!" Balling his fist, he punched her in the chest, sending her flying across the cab of the truck. She bounced with a shriek, cut short when her head hit the passenger door.

Dazed and seeing stars, Amber quickly gripped the handle on the door and held on as Tony fought for control, violently jerking the wheel as the truck sharply swerved right, then fishtailed, spewing dust clouds into the air.

"Just remember, you're making things hard on yourself!" Tony yelled, his knuckles whitening as he stomped on the brakes. The squeal of brakes assaulted her ears as the truck spun and then skidded to a dead halt, with the tail end of the bed in the middle of the road and the front bumper pointed to the ditch.

Tony threw off his seat belt and Amber quickly pulled up in the seat, still in disbelief. Angry tears burned in her eyes, but resolve kept them at bay. She would not give Tony the satisfaction of seeing her cry.

"Amber, you seem to have more lives than a cat." Tony spoke low, amusement underscoring his words as he plunged his hand into his jacket pocket. Her heart jumped to double time when she saw what he pulled out.

A laugh broke loose as Tony lifted the small plastic bag containing a syringe, capped and ready inside. "Even our feline friends run out of chances eventually."

"No!" she yelled sharply, getting ready to bolt, but there was nowhere to go. Her heart pumped so hard she could hear it in her ears. She held up her hands, palms facing him, praying he'd become reasonable. "Tony, please, let's talk about this," she pleaded, hope morphing into fear when she saw him shake his head.

"I don't think so." He grimaced.

Twisting, Amber grabbed for the door handle again and started yanking, willing, praying it would open. Her futile attempt abated as Tony grabbed a fistful of her hair and yanked her around, pushing her against the seat. She blinked up at him as he loomed over her, nausea coiling tight in her stomach.

"Relax, Amber," he whispered through clenched teeth, his hold on her hair tightening, pinning her to the seat.

As he leaned closer, rage built in her chest, but she knew it was a useless venture to try anything...yet.

"Such a shame the way things turned out," he mumbled, shaking his head, his voice softer now. "A few young men trying to have a little fun at a frat party morphed into a major disaster that continued to haunt Carl all these years. He felt so guilty when he first became my patient, and you can imagine my surprise when I heard your story and realized you were the young woman who caused him such regret."

Carl. Her heart dipped to her stomach. *So it was him.* Even more disturbing, Tony had been the one who'd counseled him.

"Carl understood it was wrong." Tony sighed. Slipping the syringe into his chest pocket, he kept talking, as if he needed time to set the record straight. "Setting you up like he did. Standing guard while his good friend Randall took you into his room, and then, of course, your near overdose, which kept Carl in fear that someday the story would find him."

"Randall," Amber said, her chest heaving. He was her college assailant, but Carl was the one who wanted her dead?

"And whether you realized it or not, you possessed the power to destroy poor Carl. His greatest fear was that you'd take your story public. And look at you," he said, shaking his head. "His fears weren't in vain. You're geared up and ready to shout your story to whole city. And once you did that, the speculation that would follow has the potential to disrupt the lives of many. Both Carl and Randall have made quite a nice career in the drug trade, thanks to me. And if either of them were investigated, my name would be sure to come out. I couldn't let that happen. I hope you understand."

Understand? Was he crazy? She wanted to squeal in protest, but when Tony let out a frustrated cry, Amber knew she needed to get out of there.

"I am sorry that things turned out like they did. If only Carl had gotten the job done right the first time. Poor man, each failed attempt weakened his resolve to follow orders and keep his mouth shut." Tony released her hair and reached for the syringe. "And now I'm forced to take care of things myself."

Panic seized Amber's throat and blood pounded in her temples. She needed to make her move, and she needed to do it now.

Before she had the chance to chicken out, she fisted her hand and punched Tony's chest, knocking him off-kilter for a second. Then she dived over the seat back of the double cab and managed to kick him in the face as he grabbed after her.

"Amber! You need to stop this!" he growled, his long arms flailing as his body dangled across the seat back.

She would never stop. Never give up. Amber grabbed on to the rear handle and pulled hard—the door flew open. But before she could scramble out, Tony lunged into the backseat and latched on to one of her ankles, dragging her across the backseat.

"I've had enough of this." He picked her up and flung her back over the front seat.

Air left her lungs as she landed with a thud. Working to regain her breath, she inhaled weakly. Each raspy breath competed with the fear flooding her chest as she caught the predatory gleam in Tony's eyes.

He was breathing heavily, impatiently, as he pulled out the syringe and ripped the plastic cap off with his teeth.

A scream wrenched from Amber's throat and bounced

off the walls of the cab. Adrenaline burned through her, but before she could work up the strength to fight, she felt the prick of the needle in her stomach.

A veil of darkness moved in. Her vision blurred and everything started to swirl. But before the shadows could swallow her up, she managed to splutter, "You'll never get away with this."

"Detective Wiley, please wait."

Patrick wasn't about to wait. Instead, he charged down the fourth-floor corridor toward the elevator, his cell phone pressed to his ear.

"You can't leave. The doctor hasn't discharged you yet." Nurse Jane stayed at his heels.

Patrick skidded to a stop at the elevator and smashed the button on the wall. He adjusted his phone to his other ear, trying to drown out the nurse's lecture and finish giving details to the police dispatcher. "Yes, Amber Talbot is likely with one of her colleagues, Tony Hill. Run his plates and track the GPS on Amber's cell phone."

"…at least stay until I contact the doctor," the nurse droned on.

Come on. Come on. Patrick kept talking to the dispatcher, willing the elevator doors to open. He punched the button again. "And put out an APB on Hill. I want every available officer looking for him." He hung up, and shot the nurse his best cop glare.

"Sorry. It's critical that I leave now."

She folded her arms, unruffled. "If you do go, we'll have to write this up as an AMA. Against medical advice. Your insurance may not pay. And…"

And if he didn't leave, Amber may not live. That concern tore at his soul. Forgetting the elevator, Patrick swung around and gave the area a quick sweep, looking for an alternative exit. He took off down the narrow hall when he spotted a glowing exit sign and the word *stairs* marked under it. He left the nurse's words trailing in his wake.

As he slammed through the door, he bit his lip against the spasm of pain that hit when his arm caught the edge of the metal door as it swung shut.

Cradling his arm to his chest, he dashed down three sets of stairs two steps at a time. Reaching the bottom, he threw open the door and burst into the lobby just as, "Code yellow, St. Joseph's Hospital. Code yellow," blared from the overhead speakers.

About time.

Patrick hastily assessed the area. A security officer stood a few yards away and was securing the glass entrance doors. His vehicle was parked outside against the curb. *Thank You, Lord.*

Patrick made a beeline for the man. "I'm with the Savannah-Chatham Police Department. Unlock the door, please, and I need the keys to your vehicle." He showed him his detective badge.

From the insipid look on the man's face, he wasn't impressed. "Sorry, sir, you'll have to take a seat." He gestured to the lobby. "Nobody can leave. We're on a lockdown."

Patrick firmly reiterated his demand, and the guard still refused.

"Why don't you radio the security office? I'll speak to them."

After a slight hesitation, the man's eyes narrowed. "Are you sure you're not a patient here?"

"Yes, I was, but I'm also a detective." Patrick flipped his badge again. "Do you carry a weapon?"

"Yes, sir. I do." The man nodded and unlocked the door, then turned back to Patrick. "I have this Taser here." He patted the holster on his belt. "Just got trained on it earlier this year."

"Never mind." Patrick quickly discounted that option.

If he got close enough to the perpetrator to use that he'd be better off relying on his hand-to-hand combat maneuvers. Even with one arm in a sling.

Patrick grabbed the keys from the guard's hand and burst out the door, grateful for the man's cooperation.

Patrick jumped behind the wheel, slammed the gearshift into Drive and floored it, not even sure exactly where he was going.

He punched in the dispatcher's number. He needed Amber's phone's GPS location.

Time to get things rolling.

Amber's eyes blinked open as the vehicle thumped and jostled over a small pothole.

Her brain was sluggish, her mouth dry. She swallowed, licked her lips and tried to get her bearings.

Twigs and branches crunched and snapped beneath the truck tires.

She tried to lift a hand to shield her eyes against the bright sunshine, but met resistance. Every platelet in her blood froze, her breath jamming in her throat. Her arms were bound behind her back, tied together with what felt like duct tape.

Adrenaline spiked, dispelling the last remnants of her unconscious state. She started to recall in horrifying detail the events of the past twenty-four hours.

Patrick had been shot. Tony wanted her dead.

Amber sucked back a sob and tried not to panic, sitting stock-still in her seat, fearful to make a sound, fearful of what Tony might do if he realized she was awake. From the corner of her eye she glimpsed him, his hands glued to the steering wheel, his neck craned as he squinted through the windshield.

Swallowing a lump of fear burning her throat, she shifted her eyes and followed his gaze. Trees came into her view, and more dense forest ahead. They were driving up an overgrown winding trail, not even a road. They were in the middle of nowhere!

Calm down, Amber. She lifted a prayer. Tony had plans to take her somewhere. He obviously didn't want to kill her in his truck or she'd be dead already.

Too messy. Too much evidence.

She was grateful. That bought her some time. When the truck door opened, that would be her chance.

She felt a smidgen better to have a fighting chance, even though the chances of getting away didn't look promising. She lifted another prayer for God's grace and mercy.

A few minutes later, at the edge of the dense woods, the trail disappeared and as they entered into a small clearing her faint glow of hope extinguished as a red four-wheel-drive truck came into view. She recognized the man leaning against the front bumper, and her heart stalled in her chest.

Randall Becker. Tall, lean and significantly more muscular than she remembered. He was wearing a Coastal Karate dark gray hoodie and matching sweats. A day's worth of beard clung to his jaw, and his eyes, dark and narrowed, stayed fixed on Tony's truck as they pulled to a stop.

Finally the missing pieces of her case started to link together, but the grim reality of what her future held settled like lead in her stomach.

It may be too late.

EIGHTEEN

Patrick sped down Highway 25 and then turned onto 170 heading toward Alligator Alley in the Savannah National Wildlife Refuge. This was where Amber's phone GPS locator device reported its approximate location. He only hoped her cell was in close proximity of her and that he wasn't too late.

He phoned Vance, huffing a sigh as he waited for him to pick up. What Patrick wouldn't give for a police radio or scanner.

Or a chance to have Amber back in his life—forever. The thought burned through him like wildfire. His heart swelled, no longer unable to deny the truth.

He loved Amber Talbot.

On the fourth ring Vance answered. "Patrick, you doing okay?"

"I'll feel better once I know Amber is safe."

"Understood. What's your location?"

"I'm about three miles from entering the wildlife refuge. What about you?"

"Not far, either." Vance's voice came back. "My ETA is about seven minutes."

"Good. I'll keep you posted on my whereabouts."

"Hold on. Before I let you go, I want to update you on something. I just got off the phone with dispatch, and the officer tailing Randall lost him about an hour ago."

"Great." Patrick's heart jumped to his throat. He jammed the gas pedal to the floor. "I'm heading in. I'll call when I know more."

"Let's go, Amber," Tony said brusquely as he yanked her by the arm, jerking her out the passenger-side door.

Before she even righted her stance, his grip bit into her arm as he dragged her around the front of his truck, directly across and several yards from where Randall stood.

Her heart dipped to her stomach. Tony, the one person who used to have the ability to calm her, now had her scared her to death.

Tension hung heavy in the air like a damp blanket as Amber waited for one of the two men to speak. The wind blowing through the field of tall grass and weeds ripped through her hair, letting stringy locks escape their bindings and slap around her face. She tossed her head, flicking hair from her eyes. She was afraid to miss anything.

"New vehicle?" Tony finally addressed Randall.

"Something like that."

"Clever. Not bringing your own. Becker, I like the way you think."

Randall didn't look amused. He lifted his square chin. "I'm not sure I like the way you think, Tony." His voice was as taut as a tripwire.

"Really? Why is that, Randall?" Tony wrenched her in front of him, clenching his arm around her waist, crushing her back against his rib cage. Was he using her as a body shield in case Randall started shooting?

Not only was Tony a creep, but he was also a coward.

A grim smile twisted Randall's features and if that gave any indication to his intentions, Tony should be worried. And so was she.

Randall came off the truck and stepped forward, one

hand never leaving his hoodie pocket. "You must think I'm stupid, Tony. I know why you called me out here today."

Tony barked a laugh, a combination of humor and annoyance. "I need your help, Randall. And like it or not, you're in this with me." He shifted a little, sank his hand into his pocket and pulled out a small gun. It was cold and hard as he held it against her back, hidden from Randall's view. She bit back a wince.

Randall snickered, then his dark eyes narrowed, became slits. "You need my help or a scapegoat?"

"Not sure what you're hinting at, Randall."

Amber bit her lip. She tempered the urge to blurt out that Tony probably had the same plans for him as he did for her. Fortunately good sense prevailed. She doubted a shared status on Tony's hit list denoted allegiance from Randall.

Randall took another step, allowing her a good look at his cold, deadly stare. "I told you from the beginning, Tony, that I didn't want anything to do with this. Carl's paranoia. Carl's deal. You knew how amped up he was, but instead of calming him down, you handed him a bomb and then had him break into Amber's house. And what did it get him? A bullet in the head."

"Carl was falling apart. He couldn't be trusted."

Amber swallowed, unnerved by the story unraveling.

"Well, now the cops are on my tail. You bought in to his stupid theory and now look at you. Everything's blown up in your face."

"Not true, Randall." Tony laughed wholeheartedly this time. "I have a wonderful scenario all figured out, you see. I was abducted along with Amber and forced to drive to the middle of no-man's-land, where miraculously I was able to overpower the abductor and get away. However, I wasn't able to save poor Amber."

Amber winced at the fabrication.

"Great story, *General*." Randall's sarcastic tone emphasized the last word. "So why don't you tell me who this abductor of yours is?"

Tony let out a hollow laugh as he whipped his pistol out and fired at Randall. "You, my friend."

Quick as lightning Randall spun and ducked. The shot burrowed into the windshield of the truck. A burst of spidery cracks splintered across it.

Randall's growl lit the air. As he raised his gun to fire back, Tony dived for cover. Amber took off in a sprint in the opposite direction, hopping over a log and running into the protection of the forest.

Gunfire exploded behind her. She dared one glance back, giving her a glimpse of Tony sprawled on the ground amid the tall grass and weeds. Randall stood beside him, his gaze whipping in every direction. Searching…for her.

Amber broke into a run, chest heaving, leaves and fallen branches crackling beneath her low-heeled shoes. Shoes not meant for hiking, much less running through the forest. She stumbled a few times, but managed to keep her footing and not fall on her face. She desperately wanted her hands free. If her footing did give way and she fell, she'd never get up. Never escape.

Randall's wild scream blended with the wind. His heavy footfalls followed her, branches and underbrush snapping beneath his feet. He was drawing closer, gaining on her.

Amber pushed forward, fighting off the terror exploding in her chest. Up ahead to the right, a steep incline came into view, and to the left was an open meadow. Exhausted and panting for breath, she was undecided for a few long seconds.

A shot rang out.

No longer concerned about escape, Amber arced to the left and entered the meadow. She needed a place to hide. Outside of a handful of towering hardwoods, the clearing was hemmed in by a mixture of short spindly pines and scrub, more like overgrown bushes than forest. Amber plunged into the line of thick foliage and ducked beneath the canopy and into the silent shadows. She caught her breath.

Plodding footsteps grew closer, followed by an irate scream. "Amber, you can't hide forever!"

Planning to prove him wrong, Amber scrambled farther into the scrub, ignoring the barbs of thorns and briars piercing her skin. Frantically, she worked to tug her hands free. The tape wouldn't budge.

Her eyes burned as desperation filled her chest. Her hands were restrained. She had nowhere to run, and a madman with a gun was on her trail. And Patrick was laid up in the hospital. No one knew she was there.

Before she could blink it away, a fat tear plopped onto her cheek. No time for pity, she reminded herself. She needed to stay strong.

Amber took a deep a breath, both to work up courage and to hold in more tears. She had to get out of there. She couldn't bear the thought of never seeing Patrick again. That was motivation enough to keep her focused.

A branch snapped behind her as the footsteps drew nearer, slowly, purposefully. Randall was in the meadow now.

She held her breath. Waited.

The footsteps ground to a stop. She stayed low and craned her head, peering through a break in the screen of bushes. Randall's mud-splotched boots came into view. He stood only few feet away, just beyond her shelter of scrub brush.

For a full minute he stood there, stiff and unpredictable. She heard his coarse and heavy breathing.

A deep and chilling terror settled over her. This was it. She held her breath. *Lord, help me.*

Ten seconds more and Randall was on the move again. *Thank You, Lord.* She was safe for the moment. Almost limp with relief, she slumped against a massive hardwood, then jerked ramrod straight when something sharp dug into her back. Twisting around, she noticed a short piece of broken branch jutting out from the tree's thick trunk.

Struck by an inspiration, she got up on her knees and worked her duct-taped wrists against the broken branch stub. Seconds passed. The tape started to rip and her heart danced.

Five minutes into the wildlife refuge on a long stretch of road, Patrick was beginning to feel as though he was on a wild-goose chase. He was in the general area of the last location Amber's cell phone had registered. But there was no guarantee that she was still in the vicinity.

Frustrated, Patrick gritted his teeth a moment before he noticed deep furrowed tire tracks veering off to the left. Someone had turned down the service track that served as a repair road for a string of high-tension power lines. Rounding the bend, he traveled down the overgrown dirt path, which was heavily rutted, making the sedan's undercarriage bottom out on every pothole in the road. He'd probably owe hospital security a new vehicle after this escapade.

Up ahead he saw a clearing, and with a squint he made out the bed of red pickup. His gut told him it was worth taking a look. He dialed Vance and gave him his location, and then pulled to the side of the road a distance from the clearing and got out. Hopefully, whoever that truck belonged to hadn't heard him.

Several minutes later, Vance's car rolled to a stop behind him. Jumping out, Vance tossed him a walkie-talkie. Patrick caught it with his good hand. "Thanks." He clipped it on his belt.

Vance slapped a pistol in his hand. "And you might be needing this. Loaded and ready."

Patrick molded his fingers around the weapon. So was he.

Patrick and Vance took off in a run and sprinted the final length of the road. Patrick gritted his teeth against the bite of pain as his arm, still in a sling, bounced against his chest.

As they entered the clearing, he saw there were two vehicles. One was Tony's truck. The red pickup he didn't recognize.

They halted. "Police! Step out where we can see you, hands raised," Vance shouted.

No reply.

Vance gestured for them to move in. They got halfway through the field when they noticed there was a man down. And it was Tony Hill.

Patrick rushed over to him. He was still alive, but bleeding from the gut.

He could hear Vance over his shoulder alerting the dispatcher, calling for a backup.

Squatting on his heels, Patrick looked into Tony's eyes. "Where's Amber?" he demanded. "Who has her?"

Tony gasped, searching for breath, his body shivering.

Patrick rubbed his shoulder. "Tony, I need you to hang in there. Can you tell me where Amber is?"

Tony swallowed hard, his gaze hollow. "Things got out of hand. I never wanted Amber hurt. Please believe me, Patrick. I…I had no choice," he managed to admit through labored breaths.

Patrick's blood began to pump harder, his heart rate picking up as he took in Tony's pallid complexion, his shallow breaths. He could see Tony was fading. He wasn't going to last long. And only he knew where Amber was, or if she was even still alive.

"Vance, we need an ambulance. Now! And I need your coat!"

"They're on the way," Vance grunted, rolling a log toward him. Patrick propped it under Tony's legs.

After Vance shed his jacket, Patrick scrunched it up and pressed it into Tony's gut, trying to slow the bleeding, trying to buy time.

"Tony, where is Amber?" Patrick asked a second time. "And who's she with? Is it Randall?"

"She ran," he choked out. "Randall...went after her."

Patrick exchanged an anxious glance with Vance.

Vance nodded and got on the radio requesting an ETA on backup and medics. Being in the boonies wasn't in their favor.

"Which way, Tony? Which direction did they head?"

Tony tried to say more, his lips moving slowly between shallow breaths. Patrick leaned closer to hear him. "What is it?"

This time when he opened his mouth, blood dribbled out. He gasped one last time, and then the shivering stopped.

Patrick felt for a pulse. The man was dead.

A grim feeling stabbed at him. Amber was somewhere in these woods, but where?

He needed to find her.

He jumped up, ignoring the electrified pain shooting through his shoulder. "Let's separate and search for Amber," he shouted at Vance.

"We have an ETA of ten minutes." Vance was right behind him. "With your injury, it might be better if we stick together."

Ten minutes was too long. "I'm good." Patrick confirmed with a nod. "I'm heading east." They needed to move quickly, to cover as much territory as possible.

"I'll go west, then. Let's hustle." Vance darted out of

sight to the left, and Patrick drove in through the trees to the right. Bracing his injured arm with his other, pistol in hand, he bolted up a small ridge. He paused to take a breath, listening, his eyes searching. He scanned the trees, the layers of the forest.

He heard leaves rustling. Groaning trees. The insistent hum of insects. Besides a skittering squirrel, nothing moved, and he saw no suspicious shadows. Nothing.

He tucked the gun into his waistband and grabbed the walkie-talkie. "Vance, what do you see?"

In response he heard static, then… "Nothing so far. You?"

"Same. Let's keep moving." Patrick clipped the radio to his belt. He glanced to his left and caught a metallic glint along the forest floor.

He went to investigate. Squatting, he picked up a silver hair clasp. *Amber's hair clasp.*

A high-pitched male shout punctuated his discovery. Angry. Vile. It had to be Randall.

Patrick whipped out his gun and started moving again, hurtling down the small hill. He was panting more than he liked, but the adrenaline pumping like fire through his veins kept him going.

His anger was amped with a heated hunger for Amber's assailant, and nothing short of stopping that creep was going to satisfy it.

Amber's pursuer was back, amped up and getting impatient. Did Randall really think his belligerent bellowing would coax her into surrendering?

She swallowed hard and lifted her eyes just enough to see over the tall weeds, peering once again through the brush. She made out Randall's serious expression as he stood in the clearing, just steps from her. He was concentrating, mumbling under his breath, his nose in the air like a hunting dog trying to catch a scent.

Gritting her teeth, she ran her hands faster, harder, against the rugged tree trunk. The tape was weakening, starting to shred. She needed to get free. It was her only hope to make it in these woods.

Her heartbeat echoed in her ears. The loud whooshing sound of her blood almost drowned out Randall's heavy footsteps as he abruptly turned and started to move again. Hopefully, he had given up and was leaving.

Please. Please. She wiggled and tugged at her hands, and the tape started to tear through. She was almost free. *Thank You, Lord!* She started again, working the tape against the broken branch stub. Up and down, sawing vigorously, weakening the integrity. But as the tape finally split apart, the ragged piece of bark caught her wrist, ripping into her flesh.

Razor-sharp pain shot up her arm, burning like fire. She swallowed hard, determined to internalize the pain, but in spite of herself, she let out a muffled shriek.

Randall's retreating steps halted. Before she could jump to her feet and take off in a run, he pivoted on his heel and came crashing through the brush, a maniacal look in his eye. The corner of his mouth hiked up in a lopsided grin as he laid eyes on her.

She swallowed, prayers flying heavenward, as she found herself staring into the barrel of his gun.

NINETEEN

As Patrick approached the clearing, anger twisted in his gut when he saw that Randall, with his gun drawn, had Amber by the arm, and was half dragging her across the open meadow. The cold determination on Randall's face said he was ready to get the job done.

Patrick turned his gaze on Amber. Her expression was riddled with fear as she stumbled along, trying to keep up with Randall's harried strides. He also saw remnants of duct tape clinging from her wrists. A combination of rage and disgust welled up in his chest.

Jaw clenched, Patrick sucked down his anger and concentrated on the job at hand. He couldn't afford to let emotion rule. It would only be an invitation to disaster. He started down a steep embankment, moving quickly but silently while scanning the area for any hint of concealed danger. With all the trees and vegetation it was easy to remain out of sight. The element of surprise would be on his side.

He needed to get into position behind Randall. As he drew closer he could hear Randall's angry words, feel the tension in the air.

"Keep moving!" Randall shoved Amber forward toward the woods. "It's time to take a little swim. The lake should be nice this time of year."

He heard a whimper from Amber. She was no doubt terrified at what was happening and what was yet to come. Patrick tried to block the emotion threatening to burst loose in him. Sweat ran down his face, tasting salty as it ran over his lips. He'd been dropped in some of the deadliest war zones in the world and had had no problem keeping his cool no matter the stimuli. Not the case today.

Patrick ducked under low-hanging branches, slipping closer into position. He checked the area one last time, noting with relief that Randall seemed to be acting alone. A surge of excruciating pain shot through the gash in his shoulder. Gritting his teeth, he ignored it. He'd been trained to push past pain and get the job done. He slipped out of the camouflage of the trees, treading softly into position behind Randall.

Three steps. Four. On the fifth… "Let her go," Patrick said, keeping his voice even, his gun perfectly steady and trained on Randall.

Randall jerked around, holding Amber tightly against him, his gun to her head. His eyes grew wide, then twinkled as they roamed over Patrick's injured arm. "Looking a bit mangled there, Wiley," Randall said with a laugh that was more frigid than polar ice. "And since when did I start taking orders from you?"

"Since right about now." Patrick took a small step toward him. "Since I have the ability to blow you away from right where I stand."

Randall cocked his gun with a click and pressed it harder against Amber's temple. "And the moment you shoot, *bang*, Amber's dead. It's called the domino effect."

Turbulent green eyes stared back at him, wide with fear, pleading for help. She trembled so hard that the tattered sleeves of her torn jacket shook, and Patrick's blood ran cold.

Battling to hold on to his composure, Patrick struggled

to slow his heart rate and eased a step closer. "And if you kill her, Becker, you'll die on the spot, you know that, so do us both a favor and lower your weapon." Patrick held his gun to his side as a sign of good faith.

Randall didn't budge.

"Come on, Randall, we're at an impasse here. If you want to live, let's make a deal. Let Amber go and I'll do whatever you want."

He could see the veins in Randall's neck bunching as he thought about it. "Okay," he said after a moment. "Drop your gun and I'll let her go." The muscles in Randall's arms visibly tensed as he tightened his grip around Amber's waist.

Patrick took a deep breath. Randall wasn't very convincing, and Patrick was running out of patience. Being reasonable didn't seem possible here.

"That's what I thought." Randall snorted. "See, already I don't trust you."

Ditto. Patrick needed a distraction, needed an opportunity to move in without getting Amber hurt. As he lifted a prayer, he cut a glance Amber's way, made eye contact. She blinked twice, as if signaling him that she had read his mind.

He tracked the bead of sweat trickling from her hairline. The rapid rise and fall of her chest. She was ready. He hoped.

"Okay." Patrick shifted his gaze to Randall. "We need to come up with a compromise. I'm open to suggestions."

A smirked slipped across Randall's face, and Amber sucked in a sharp gasp as he forced the gun harder against her temple. "Let me walk out of here with Amber. Once I get a safe distance away, I'll release her."

Yeah, right. Randall was even crazier than he thought. Irritation danced across Patrick's nerve endings. Mind reeling, he grappled for a plan. And judging by the predatory gleam in Randall's eyes, he was doing the same.

The radio clipped to his belt crackled as a coarse, staticky voice broke the stalemate. "Wiley, do you copy?"

Startled by the sound, Randall jerked. His grip on Amber suddenly went slack, and she flung herself out of his grasp.

"No, you don't!" Randall was as quick as a striking snake as he launched after her and latched on to her arm.

As Amber's scream penetrated the air, Patrick broke into a run and threw all his weight up against Randall.

With a scream, Randall staggered back several feet and Patrick wheeled around, teeth clenched, looking for the weapon he'd just lost.

"Got you!" A laugh burst from Randall's throat as he swung his pistol into position.

A shot erupted from the barrel, and Patrick lurched to the side, the bullet blasting past the left side of his head.

Screams of terror rang out from Amber. Patrick didn't give Randall a chance to fire again. He jumped forward with a quick roundhouse kick, sending Randall's gun flying.

Randall retaliated with a spinning jump kick that Patrick blocked, then came at him with a flurry of high-speed punches.

Blocking and ducking, he felt adrenaline thrash through his body like lightning. Using his uninjured arm, he swung a hook punch at Randall's head.

Randall jumped out of the way. "I hope you like dirt! Because I plan to grind your face into it!" Then with a loud "Kiai!" he snapped a kick toward Patrick's head.

"Nope, sure don't." Patrick ducked his head and spun forward with a jumping front kick of his own that slammed against Randall's ribs.

Randall spun around and lunged at him with a right-left

combination that landed a sharp blow to Patrick's head and had him stumbling into the tree line. Pivoting quickly, he barely missed another roundhouse kick to the head.

Now Patrick was done playing. He spun forward with a reverse side kick and slammed his boot against Randall's head, sending his adversary crashing onto his back.

Chest heaving, Randall flipped back to his feet and snapped into a fighting stance. "Wiley! You're mine!"

Winded and feeling dizzy, Patrick clenched his teeth against the torturous pain in his shoulder. Dismissing it, he focused on his opponent with a single goal in mind—take him down and get Amber out of there.

Before that thought fully processed, Randall pounced forward and came at him with a series of kicks. Patrick spun, bobbed and weaved, pivoted and ducked. Out of the corner of his eye he saw Amber swoop up his pistol and try to aim. Her hands shook wildly. His already galloping heart rate doubled. Being brave was great, but now she was dangerous. One misfire could do him in, and then Randall would easily overtake her.

The distraction cost Patrick as the tip of Randall's boot caught him in the shoulder. Pain shot through every nerve ending, followed by a shudder that rocked his whole body. Anger competed with adrenaline as Patrick shielded Randall's next kick and slammed a palm-heel strike against his chest, sending Randall skidding back into a tree.

With the last of his energy, Patrick rushed to Amber, grabbed the pistol from her. He pulled her against him and trained the gun on Randall. "You doing okay?" he whispered against the top of her head.

Nodding, Amber clung to him.

In the distance he saw police officers break through the tree line, Vance in the lead. The cavalry had finally arrived.

Better late than never. Patrick eyed Randall, who was

struggling to breathe, slumped against the tree. He was trying to slow down his own breath. If Randall knew what was good for him, he'd better not budge. Patrick's patience had seriously run dry.

As Amber settled more firmly against him, a lump rose in Patrick's throat. The thought that he could have lost her today sent chills up his spine.

"I'm glad you're okay," he whispered to her. "I've never been so afraid."

"Me, either," she said, and let out a hoarse sob.

"I realized something today." He brushed a kiss on the top of her head.

"What's that?" There was a slight tremor in her voice.

"That I never want to lose you again."

Amber didn't move, didn't respond.

"God put you back in my life, Amber. And I don't think it was just to set your past straight and bring this creep to justice." He eyed Randall still working to breathe as Vance slapped on his cuffs.

She stayed silent but nestled closer to him, and his heart swelled to almost bursting as he waited for her to respond. Surely she couldn't deny that they were meant for each other.

Finally, she drew in a deep breath. "I want to believe that, Patrick. But can you forgive me for all the pain I caused you?"

"I already have," he said. "I love you, Amber."

After a moment, she raised her eyes to his. "I love you, too, Patrick," Amber whispered through her tears. "I never stopped loving you."

Oh, yeah. He smiled. Nothing had ever sounded better to him.

EPILOGUE

One week later

After all the months of planning, the Silence No More fund-raiser had finally arrived.

Standing beneath the glimmering reception hall chandeliers, overlooking a myriad of guests, Amber spoke candidly about her personal experience, sharing the ordeal she'd gone through, wanting other victims to know they were not alone and that help was available.

"It is time to speak out and raise awareness about the issue of abuse and violence against women. A crime that strikes one in three women, many of whom continue to live in the shadows, feeling the shame and guilt that victims of abuse feel. A place I've been myself."

Amber paused, tears welling in her eyes. "I want to encourage all victims to become survivors. It's time to break the silence, the first step in healing."

The audience rose, giving Amber a standing ovation at the completion of her speech. She remembered a time when talking about the past would have been impossible. God's grace was incredible.

Standing in the back of the reception hall, Amber helped Kim match the list of silent auction winners with gift baskets they'd won as the guests were enjoying dessert. The evening had just about come to an end, and things couldn't have gone better.

"You did great." The deepest, most charming timbre sounded in her ear as Patrick swept his arm around her, pulling her close.

She glanced up at him, smiling. "Thank you."

He skimmed a kiss across her temple. "If you have a minute, I have something I need to talk to you about."

"All right." She had all the time in the world for this man. She handed Kim the list of names and followed him through a set of double doors into the small corridor overlooking the twinkling lights of Savannah's skyline.

Amber locked gazes with Patrick, and automatically her heart swelled. "What did you want to talk to me about?"

A half grin curved the side of his mouth. "I want to tell you how proud I am of you. Telling your story is going to help so many."

She nearly dissolved into tears right there. "Thank you." For the first time in forever, she felt free. Free from the bonds of guilt. Ready to live. Ready to love. Her heart danced. *Thank You, Lord.*

"And…" He fished something out of his pocket. "I have something to give back to you."

As she tried to figure what he had of hers, he opened his hand, and what she saw resting in his palm stole her breath.

A ring. But not just any platinum princess-cut diamond solitaire.

Her ring.

The tears she'd tried to keep at bay now streamed down her cheeks. All these years, he'd kept her ring.

Her perfect evening got even better.

Patrick stepped closer and swept her into his embrace.

His mouth closed over hers in a kiss so tender, so sweet, it assured her that his heart belonged to her.

And hers belonged to him. Forever.

* * * * *

Dear Reader,

I hoped you enjoyed reading about Patrick and Amber in *Broken Silence*. Reunited love stories are such fun to write, especially with a little suspense sprinkled in.

Like many of us, Patrick and Amber battle with scars from the past. But Amber's secret keeps her on a roller coaster of fear and regret, and in the process weakens her faith. As hard as she tried to cover her pain by helping other women victims of abuse, her only way to freedom is to let go of the past and put her faith back in God.

Patrick is a man whose faith continues to grow, although he still struggles to open his heart to love, for fear of getting hurt again. So when Patrick's and Amber's worlds collide and they work together to unravel the truth of the past, they also learn valuable lessons about trust, forgiveness and love.

Remember, through God all things are possible!

I love to hear from my readers. You can email me at annsleeurban@gmail.com, and to find out more about me and my books, please visit me at annsleeurban.com!

Annslee

COMING NEXT MONTH FROM
Love Inspired® Suspense

Available April 7, 2015

DUTY BOUND GUARDIAN
Capitol K-9 Unit • by Terri Reed

A stolen art relic leads K-9 officer Adam Donovan to Lana Gomez as the prime suspect. Yet when the true thief tries to kill Lana, Adam must safeguard the gorgeous museum curator.

SECRET REFUGE
Wings of Danger • by Dana Mentink

The man who killed Keeley Stevens's sister is now threatening Keeley. Former parole officer Mick Hudson knows it's up to him to keep her out of harm's way and bring the criminal to justice.

TARGETED • by Becky Avella

Despite his recent injury, officer Rick Powell is determined to keep schoolteacher Stephanie O'Brien from becoming a serial killer's next victim.

ROYAL RESCUE • by Tammy Johnson

Ever since her father's murder, princess Thea James has lived in fear. Royal bodyguard Ronin Parrish promises he'll shield her from the attacker, but does he have ulterior motives?

PRESUMED GUILTY • by Dana R. Lynn

Framed for a crime she did not commit, Melanie Swanson must now trust a handsome policeman to protect her from becoming the real criminal's next target.

FATAL FREEZE • by Michelle Karl

Trapped aboard an icebound ferry with a dangerous crime ring, private investigator Lexie Reilly and undercover CIA agent Shaun Lane will need to work together if they want to survive.

LISCNM0315

REQUEST YOUR FREE BOOKS!

2 FREE RIVETING INSPIRATIONAL NOVELS
PLUS 2 FREE MYSTERY GIFTS

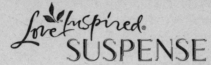

YES! Please send me 2 FREE Love Inspired® Suspense novels and my 2 FREE mystery gifts (gifts are worth about $10). After receiving them, if I don't wish to receive any more books, I can return the shipping statement marked "cancel." If I don't cancel, I will receive 4 brand-new novels every month and be billed just $4.74 per book in the U.S. or $5.24 per book in Canada. That's a savings of at least 21% off the cover price. It's quite a bargain! Shipping and handling is just 50¢ per book in the U.S. and 75¢ per book in Canada.* I understand that accepting the 2 free books and gifts places me under no obligation to buy anything. I can always return a shipment and cancel at any time. Even if I never buy another book, the two free books and gifts are mine to keep forever.

123/323 IDN F5AC

Name	(PLEASE PRINT)	

Address		Apt. #

City	State/Prov.	Zip/Postal Code

Signature (if under 18, a parent or guardian must sign)

Mail to the Harlequin® Reader Service:
IN U.S.A.: P.O. Box 1867, Buffalo, NY 14240-1867
IN CANADA: P.O. Box 609, Fort Erie, Ontario L2A 5X3

**Are you a current subscriber to Love Inspired Suspense books
and want to receive the larger-print edition?
Call 1-800-873-8635 or visit www.ReaderService.com.**

* Terms and prices subject to change without notice. Prices do not include applicable taxes. Sales tax applicable in N.Y. Canadian residents will be charged applicable taxes. Offer not valid in Quebec. This offer is limited to one order per household. Not valid for current subscribers to Love Inspired Suspense books. All orders subject to credit approval. Credit or debit balances in a customer's account(s) may be offset by any other outstanding balance owed by or to the customer. Please allow 4 to 6 weeks for delivery. Offer available while quantities last.

Your Privacy—The Harlequin® Reader Service is committed to protecting your privacy. Our Privacy Policy is available online at www.ReaderService.com or upon request from the Harlequin Reader Service.
We make a portion of our mailing list available to reputable third parties that offer products we believe may interest you. If you prefer that we not exchange your name with third parties, or if you wish to clarify or modify your communication preferences, please visit us at www.ReaderService.com/consumerschoice or write to us at Harlequin Reader Service Preference Service, P.O. Box 9062, Buffalo, NY 14269. Include your complete name and address.

LIS13R

SPECIAL EXCERPT FROM

Love Inspired
SUSPENSE

Framed for a crime she didn't commit,
museum curator Lana Gomez must prove her
innocence under the watchful eyes of
Capitol K-9 Unit officer Adam Donovan.

Read on for a sneak preview of
the next exciting installment of the
CAPITOL K-9 UNIT *series,*
DUTY BOUND GUARDIAN
by *Terri Reed.*

K-9 officer Adam Donovan's cell buzzed inside the breast pocket of his uniform shirt. He halted, staying out of the rain beneath the overhang covering the entrance to the E. Barrett Prettyman Federal Courthouse.

"Sit," he murmured to his partner, Ace, a four-year-old, dark-coated, sleek Doberman pinscher. The dog obediently sat on his right. Keeping Ace's lead in his left hand, he answered the call. "Adam Donovan."

By habit Adam scanned the crowds of tourists flooding the National Mall, on alert for any criminal activity. Not even nighttime or an April drizzle could keep sightseers in their hotels. To his right the central dome of the US Capitol building gleamed with floodlights, postcard perfect.

"Gavin here" came the deep voice of his boss, Captain Gavin McCord. "You still at the courthouse?"

Adam had had a late meeting with the DA regarding a case against a drug dealer who'd been selling in and around the metro DC area. The elite Capitol K-9 Unit had been called in to assist the local police during a two-hour manhunt nine months ago. The K-9 unit was often enlisted in various crimes throughout the Washington, DC, area.

Ace had been the one to find the suspect hiding in a construction Dumpster outside of the National Gallery of Art. The suspect took the DA's deal and gave up the names of his associates rather than stand trial, which had been scheduled to begin later this week.

A victory on this rainy spring evening.

"Yes, sir."

"There's been a break-in at the American Museum and two of the museum employees have been assaulted," Gavin stated.

"Injured or dead?" Adam asked, already moving down the steps toward his vehicle with Ace at his heels.

"Injured. The intruder rendered both employees unconscious, but the security guard came to and pulled the fire alarm, scaring off the intruder. Both have been rushed to the hospital on Varnum Street." Gavin's tone intensified. "But the other victim is who I'm interested in. Lana Gomez."